Tumbleweed and Dreams
A Novel by T. P. Graf

Book I
From the Trilogy - The Life and Stories of Jaime Cruz

This is a work of fiction. While some of the public places and
institutions exist and events in relation to time may be real, the
characters and context involved are wholly imaginary. The
opinions expressed are those of the characters and should not be
confused with those of the author.

This trilogy is dedicated to
the generous hearts and beautiful creatures
living under the vast West Texas skies.

Writings of T.P. Graf

As the Daisies Bloom - A Novel

PenCraft Awards - 2020 First Place, Cultural Fiction
Book Excellence Awards - 2021 Finalist, Friendship
Chanticleer IBA, 2020 First Place, Somerset Book Awards

A beautiful telling of life's trials and tribulations, always overcome by the love of family and of something greater than oneself. - Reader's Favorite

Enchanting as it is charming ... intimately and poetically told ... like a well-written symphony - Literary Titan

A powerfully written character-led novel; stark and unsettling but often funny too. Highly recommended! - A 'Wishing Shelf' Book Review

August Kibler's Stories for Tyler
Voices of Context from Eden to Patmos
(Companion to As the Daisies Bloom)

Firebird Award - 2021 Winner, Christian Poetry
American Book Awards - 2021 Finalist, Religious Poetry
Royal Dragonfly, 2021 Honorable Mention, Religion/Spirituality

A compelling and thought-provoking study of the bible and Christian history. The writing style is almost angelic! It's the sort of book you want to discuss; that stays with you for a long, long time.
- A 'Wishing Shelf' Book Review

Graf has crafted a masterful work of modern literature that takes on some very complex topics...in a format that any reader can engage with and glean wisdom from ... entertaining ... highly recommend.
- Reader's Favorite

The book offers fresh ideas ... absorbing ... thought-provoking and evokes a positive emotional connotation. - Literary Titan

Roots, Branches and Buzz Saws
More Stories of August Kibler

"Celebrate who you are, even if it is quietly...". That is what this book is, a celebration of August's life and a reminder to the reader to celebrate their life, who they are. - Literary Titan

Looking Out onto Our World
Explorations of Power, Dogma and
a World Deserving of Contemplation

The Life and Stories of Jaime Cruz (Trilogy)

Tumbleweed and Dreams (Book One)
From the Series - The Life and Stories of Jaime Cruz

Graf manages to keep readers enthralled with Jaime's day-to-day experiences chapter after chapter ... a beautifully penned tale of self-discovery and a strong main character who stands out in a crowd.
- Literary Titan

A gripping story filled with colorful and often captivating characters.
- A 'Wishing Shelf' Book Review

An immersive journey of self-discovery and a sense of home ... you find yourself invested in the lives of the people and the friendships that are made. - Readers' Favorite

Night Air Descending (Book Two)
From the Series - The Life and Stories of Jaime Cruz

A cleverly-crafted, character-led family drama set in Texas. I got so immersed in it, I started to feel like one of the family too!
- A 'Wishing Shelf' Book Review

Whether you're in the mood for a slice-of-life drama or a study of eclectic characters, Night Air Descending by T.P. Graf is a memorable read.
- Readers' Favorite

This is a beautifully written book that has a grounded and authentic feel so much that it feels like we are reading someone's diary ... heartwarming ... [with a] distinct literary aesthetic. - Literary Titan

Seeds in the Desert Wind (Book Three)
From the Series - The Life and Stories of Jaime Cruz

Every quirk, every nuance, and each daily challenge make this story relatable and enjoyable...a book that wraps around you like your favorite blanket and touches your heart in a unique way. - Literary Titan

Graf again delivers interesting, full-bodied characters that we can relate to and want to follow through to their conclusions... a story that will entertain and move you. - Readers' Favorite

A powerful, often thought-provoking end to this excellent trilogy. Highly recommended. - A 'Wishing Shelf' Book Review

A Cowgirl's Stories
Companion to The Life and Stories of Jaime Cruz Trilogy

Sallie is such a special character ... I adore that readers do not necessarily know where Sallie will take us next. The unpredictability of her tales is endearing in the best possible way. - Literary Titan

You'll certainly be hooked on the attitude and atmosphere of the world so lovingly crafted. - Readers' Favorite

A richly textured and often humorous story of a life growing up in Texas ... full of revelations and insights into a totally different world.
- The 'Wishing Shelf' Book Review

Days in the Desert
Food for Body and Soul

Delicious and nutritious! - Reader Review

Part I

Chapter One

When I headed south on I-5 towards I-10, I didn't know if I was running from something or to something. The only thing I seemed to know as I looked back in my rearview mirror was that anything back there wasn't going to come with me to where I was going—not if I could help it. The little I had, I sold in California before I left in the pickup that was now to be the only home I might know for a time. The old brown Ford Ranger, if I was lucky, would get me to where I was headed without breaking down. If she did break down, then the little money I did have from the sale of my non-essentials would be quickly lost. Fourteen hundred more miles seemed like a lot for the pickup with almost two hundred thousand miles. I guessed if she didn't make it to West Texas, I would just have to stay where she died and hope to find something to earn a little money to get by. It's not like my Texas plan was much more defined than that anyway.

The new millennium for me would begin in a new place. That was all I really knew of my future. I had no job to go to. No relative at the other end that could offer me a place to stay while I got back on my feet. I was facing the hard reality that my life had not gone to plan. Now, I didn't even have a plan. I saw the movie *Dancer, Texas, Pop. 81* and decided that as those boys left for California, I would leave for "Dancer." Crazy, isn't it?

"Dancer" was a made-up place. I had to go somewhere real. According to the movie credits that real place was Fort Davis. You can't call what I was doing in any way a plan. I had no illusion that I could blend into a small community and live in my pickup as one can do in a larger urban area. But I had had enough of urban life and took as a kind of faith that things would work out somehow if I could just get to a new place and start a new life.

There was no money for motels along the way, and I wasn't going to waste any money on eating out. I made a few provisions for food that I could take with me and would sleep as I needed to along the highways' rest areas. Hopefully, I wouldn't be harassed. Certainly, I had little concern for being robbed as one look at the pickup would have suggested to any competent thief that robbing me would be a wasted effort—not worth any risk of arrest. The only things I possessed in any quantity at that time were depression and worry. Plenty of things were in short supply—everything that most would consider essential.

I had a few things going for me. I was on the very bottom side of my thirties and had no chronic health problems. I was male, and I was straight. And while my last name was Cruz, I could pass for white easily enough. My mother's gringa and father's Spanish roots, with little of the darker Central American indigenous blood, made me as white-looking as most of my American Caucasian brothers and sisters. While "my kind" might not elicit sympathy from many, I also knew I was unlikely to suffer the sexual, racial and bigoted treatment some other mix of characteristics might bring on in such a risky trip as I was setting out on.

My sin, if you want to call it that, was good old business failure. I had tried to make it in a small business and failed miserably. All confidence was gone. The failure so abject, I let my pride drive me into despair. California represents a certain apex of America as the land of more. It is a beautiful place until you have no money. It was hard to imagine a way out of the hole I'd dug myself into. I knew I could try to stay and get some low-paying job, but that wasn't going to be a real solution either. All I could play in my mind was the Gatlin Brothers' song *All the gold in California is in a bank in the middle of Beverly Hills in somebody else's name....Tryin' to be a hero, winding up a zero, can scar a man forever right down to your soul...* That seemed to be my theme song, and I *desperately* needed a new one.

I was also under no illusion that life in a new place was going to be easy or some fast track to security. Quite the opposite. I viewed the move to the Texas desert as both escape and a certain resignation to living on the margins of life where such a life still seemed possible in this land of more. Fort Davis was the first stop on that quest, but I knew it might well lead me deeper into the Big Bend region, where others had gone to escape "civilization" in favor of seclusion and a minimalist material existence.

There are those in the religious life who take on a form of what they refer to as voluntary poverty. In some cases their poverty seems real enough, and they serve the poor in ways that ought to inspire us to lives of sacrificial service. Some, to me, look more like they retreat from the world within the cloister with their security in a beautiful edifice owned by a well-established order. If simple around the edges of their religious lifestyle, the monastic life is not a bad life when taken in whole. Well, my poverty was not voluntary, and I certainly had no support organization to give me security within any cloister. If I was going to resemble anything in the tradition of the religious, it appeared to me my life would resemble more the life of the desert fathers and mothers who quite literally moved into the desert and lived a non-materialistic life few can fathom. I would let their example wander through my mind as I merged onto I-5 for that long trip from the land of more to the far more barren desert.

Those imaginings both frightened me and appealed to me at the same time. I'd learned that humiliation and humility have nothing in common. I was living with humiliation—a direct result of my ego and pride, which had been decimated by my failures. When some unknown stranger, either accidentally or purposely, left a book in my place of business on the desert fathers and mothers that Thomas Merton had assembled, *The Wisdom of the Desert*, I began to digest just what the fruits of humility might actually look like in one's life. It certainly was the contra-lifestyle to everything I had tried to aspire to, and for that matter, to which everyone around me seemed to aspire. Where others succeeded in their aspirations, I had failed.

The one grace of my failure, as I saw it, was that it was a solitary affair. There was no wife nor any children who had to be drug down into despair with me. My few relationships to date had the same fundamental flaws my business dealings seemed to possess. The only degree of humility I can claim in all this was the fact that I knew I was the problem and never blamed others for my failures. It didn't make the pill any easier to swallow, but at least the pain I transmitted to others was minimal compared to what it might have been had I been in greater denial—blaming everyone *but* myself.

No, I was the problem plain and simple, and I and the rest of the world seemed to know it.

Every few hundred miles I would pull into rest stops for a peanut butter fold-over, some water, a pit stop and read a few pages from that book before I'd hit the road again with the same hope that the old brown Ford would keep running.

The abbas and ammas of the desert in Merton's book clearly had some faith that I couldn't really comprehend. I wasn't religious. I was not a believer, agnostic or atheist. Each of those would have required some due diligence of thought that I had never given to the subject. As I drove towards the desert, the logical middle of agnosticism lodged in my mind as some explanation I might consider since the other two ends of the spectrum, it seemed to me, each required a great leap of faith. Atheism required the commitment to certainty that I was unwilling to consider. The world's religions, as I had observed from the outside, depended as well on this commitment to certainty. The only certainties I held at the moment were that I had certainly failed in the American dream, and I certainly needed a new start if I was ever going to emerge from this depression without ending my life by my own hand.

With the passing miles, I'd begun to formulate an alternative life. When I first decided I would head to "Dancer," I very much imagined looking for work and slowly but surely rebuilding a very conventional lifestyle. Someday, I would be married with a family living happily in my three bedroom house in or near Fort Davis. I would achieve a modest version of the American dream that had eluded me in California. For the first time in my life, I imagined it without the dreams of success in its various trappings. Was it possible to live a marginal existence in the desert with a complete detachment from the materialism of our culture? Perhaps those desert monastics were a one-off. Much of history since their time in the desert would suggest such was the case. I thought how people weren't exactly lining up to live as they had. World religions never embraced their ethos as informing their own polity—that much was pretty clear to me even without any religious experience or study on my part.

As I drove along the Rio Grande communities east of El Paso, I envisioned each as some small community of humble farmers and laborers eking out a living without the trappings of success weighing them down. I knew it was not that simplistic in those villages off I-10, but it fostered an imagination for a life I'd not given a second's thought to ever before. There is no denying the poverty along the border—even more so across the river into Mexico. It was anything but voluntary. At the same time, it would be a disservice to their dignity to suggest that they haven't taken life as it has come to them and done their best to maintain a community of care for each other that can be next to impossible to find in the self-centered urban life. In that regard, it was *not* a stretch to imagine these small villages and surrounding farms as a type of desert monasticism in its more contemporary form with their Ford and Chevy pickups and satellite TVs.

Chapter Two

With "pay at the pump" and my rest-stop dining and napping, I had managed the past twenty-four hours without speaking to another soul. I never turned on the radio. The only voices were the ones in my head—from my own thoughts and fears and those of desert monastics from the page. By the time I got to Fort Davis, I was no longer sure what my next step might be. I'd assumed I'd just find some place to park, and do my best to keep myself clean with the dry-bath makings I'd brought with me until I could get work somewhere and find some hovel to rent.

My first impressions of the area around Fort Davis were more than positive. The landscape gave me the first real feeling of peace I'd had in a long time. Perhaps it's not an exaggeration to say, ever. Since I had never oriented my thoughts to anything other than the material prosperity of California, it is fair to say that I never looked for simplicity there though it surely exists in some form. Here the desert mountains and the sparse development grabbed me in a way that had been teased in my movie watching of *Dancer, Texas*—but was now far more acute in my first encounter with the place than I had imagined possible. I had the oddest sense that somehow I belonged.

I couldn't afford to just drive around and burn the little bit of money I had in my gas-guzzling Ford. I would first scope out Fort Davis, and if no jobs were available, I'd go looking for some job in Alpine. Could be there were more housing options as well as job options in the larger Alpine town anyway. As far as Fort Davis, it looked to me like the biggest employer was probably the large greenhouse, though I had no idea what they were growing. It seemed such a strange place for such a huge agricultural endeavor. I figured they paid little but probably always needed help. I also imagined that, as with much of California agriculture, the help probably was heavily Hispanic, and the fact that I was bilingual to a degree might be of some benefit. Maybe I'd start there. If I could get a greenhouse job, at least it might afford me some little bit of money coming in to live on. It was too late in the day to do anything about that now. I found a place to park where I thought no one would take notice and would get as good a night's sleep as possible.

I arrived early the next morning as vans were pulling in coming from the south. I wondered if these were workers being brought in from Mexico, which was still almost two hours to the south, or if they were from some labor camp compound somewhere. Whichever it was, it was pretty clear a lot of the workers were being brought in en masse. The guard directed me to a place to park and where I needed to go to apply for a job. He called someone inside to make them aware of my impending arrival so they could let me in. Security seemed to be pretty tight for such a remote business as this. I'd begun to wonder if they were doing some kind of government research. That would explain the remoteness of the operation and the tight security.

The first real amusement I'd had in months came when I was given a quick tour of the place and discovered my imagined, top secret research facility was in fact a hothouse tomato farm owned by the Dutch. They also operated an even larger facility just down the road about ten miles. My employment wasn't going to require an FBI clearance. It was clear if I was offered a job, I could begin as soon as I was willing. It was equally clear that being bilingual *was* going to be as helpful as I thought it *might* be as most workers were from Mexico in addition to Fort Davis locals.

They don't call them hothouse tomatoes for nothing! That place was hot, but impressive. They had technology to feed the plants C02 and heating pipes for winter that doubled as rails for their work platforms that they could raise and lower to trim the vines and harvest the fruit. Each plant was set in a hydroponic mineral wool trays and trained as a large "V" tied up to form a lattice look with the other vines. Beneficial insect boxes were scattered around the hot-house, and the fruit was packaged and loaded into semi-trailers for sale as far away as Florida. The manager had me taste one of their tomatoes. I was surprised. It actually tasted like a tomato—not the hard tasteless kind I'd grown accustomed to in the supermarkets I frequented.

It was such a relief that an honest accounting of how and why I came to Fort Davis was enough to get me hired. The pay was about what I expected, but that was fine by me. I didn't take any chances by turning this down in hopes of some better opportunity. I needed work, and I took it. They were happy for me to start that same day, and so I did. A man from Fort Davis who had worked there for many years was retiring. I wasn't to have his job as another employee was moving up into his supervisory role. Still, I was lucky enough to get the promoted person's position in running part of the packing lines, which meant being in the cooler part of the operation. There was the customary paperwork to be filled out, which took all of twenty minutes tops, and I was put to work. With the help of the man whose job I was taking, I was able to talk with those who lived in or near Fort Davis to see if any knew of a place I could rent. I made it clear I'd have to wait for my first paycheck in order to do so.

One of the employees, Chuy Cardona, had a little apartment that was empty and, as he described it, was "pretty rough around the edges." I assured him I wasn't looking for a luxury accommodation and would like to see it if I could. He suggested I follow him home after work, which I did. He was right. It was rough and tiny, but it had a bed, bathroom, hot plate and the size refrigerator you find in some motels. The rent would be $250 a month with bills paid. It didn't have an air conditioner, just a swamp cooler, which he assured me was all that was generally needed in Fort Davis. He was kind enough to let me move in right then and pay him when I got paid.

Chuy's wife, Lupita, came to see what her husband was up to.

Just as I had at the tomato farm, I introduced myself in the Spanish pronunciation of my first name, which I'd never done before today. "I'm *Jaime* Cruz. I just arrived from California."

"I'm Lupe," she responded. "How does someone from California end up in Fort Davis?"

I gave an honest answer if not a complete one. "That, I'm not sure I really know the answer to. Only time will tell." I hoped they wouldn't press me for a more thorough telling, and neither did.

She loaned me a set of sheets and a blanket and a couple towels until I could get to Alpine to buy my own things. She turned the small hot water heater on and left me to make myself at home.

It was hard to believe that less than twenty-four hours earlier, I had driven into a new town—picked out by watching a movie once upon a time—with no prospect of work or a home. Now, though many would consider both low-grade options, I was employed and housed. And while there was a time I would have felt a degree of humiliation at my present situation, I instead found myself incredibly at peace.

The few things in the pickup were unloaded, and I feasted on my staple of peanut butter and bread; only this time I opened my one jar of sweet pickles to add to my sandwich. I had enough of each of these to last me until payday, and I knew I had enough money to get some eggs, bacon and a few other items from the local grocery store. Right after I finished my dinner I hopped in the shower and felt the warm water wash away all the anxiety and fear that had been with me for the last several months. As I went to bed, I opened again *The Wisdom of the Desert*. There I read,

If you see a young monk by his own will climbing up to heaven, take him by the foot and throw him to the ground, because what he is doing is not good for him.

It struck me how much I had tried to climb on my own. Circumstance, or so it seemed, threw me to the ground. In the shabby room, I uttered what was my first real prayer in my life. I simply said, "Thank you for this day, and grant me a peaceful night." I didn't know if I was praying to a god or to the cosmos or if there was any difference between those two. There was simply some compunction to acknowledge the chance that some force of love existed that I had ignored to my detriment.

My request was granted, and I woke up with something I'd not known before—hope. I realized how much I'd allowed baseless optimism to prop me up and a growing, persistent pessimism to tear me down—all the while never really knowing any sense of hope.

I was determined to take the job as it came and wasn't worried about advancing or getting a raise. I would take on a new discipline for me, which was to live within my means however frugal that might require. It wasn't laziness that brought me to this situation. It was more my pride than anything else—hanging on to a lost cause rather than admit defeat. This job offered me a chance to work with others in the simplest kind of mutual respect if I could earn their respect. And so I set out from day one to fit in, work hard, never complain and leave the day grateful for another day's labor.

My now landlord and fellow worker suggested we ride to work together. I'm sure he wondered about the life expectancy of the old Ranger. I quickly accepted his offer and told myself I would give him gas money each payday in return for his driving.

When payday came, I paid my rent for the month and gave Chuy some money for gas. Then I drove down to Alpine to get the bed and bath items I needed to allow me to wash and return what had been loaned to me. Back in Fort Davis, I went to the grocery store and got enough to get me to another payday.

I'd heard from others at work that there was a food pantry in town, which I was told was run very efficiently by a woman who first organized it to serve the entire county. I was pretty sure I would qualify for food, but decided to first go to the Saturday distributions and volunteer to help. They had a great group of volunteers and the chief organizer who ran it was most welcoming. As a single-person household at my current wages, I did qualify for food—but for the time being, I decided to wait and just help out most distribution days. It was a great way to get to know both the volunteers and the people the pantry was serving. Being bilingual was appreciated and as helpful to me as it was to them. Working at the pantry helped me appreciate just how much my marginal life was relatable to so many in this border community. The kindness and basic dignity that were evident was a kind of elixir for me. I felt myself healing day by day, and finding the fears and failures of my years in California as an increasingly distant abstraction.

After two months at work, I was comfortable with everyone there and they were comfortable with me. I know all jobs carry the risk of downsizing and dismissal, and I would never assume myself immune from that possibility. Until it happened, I would take one day at a time, save what little I could from my meager earnings and continue to live in the one room apartment so long as they'd have me. I would read from that book mysteriously left for me and repeat my prayer each night as I went to bed.

Chapter Three

My life in the desert was about as simple as it gets. I didn't have a TV, phone or computer. I thought perhaps I should get a phone, but for what? If I was ill and needed to let the greenhouse know, my landlord would take care of that on my behalf. There certainly was no one in California I wanted to talk to. I was estranged from friends and family long before leaving the state. I wasn't eager to add to my monthly expenses for big-ticket items like a computer or TV, and so I lived without. I did get a library card and began checking out a few books to read in my off hours.

I found a couple more by Thomas Merton though I have to confess that his depth in the Christian life was largely going over my head. Still, it gave me something to contemplate, and he began to teach me the value of silence. In this place it seemed natural to turn off one's mind for the experience of just sitting quietly.

I got a cheap lawn chair, and in the evenings would just sit and stare towards the Davis Mountains' rocky outcroppings that were visible from my little hovel. I decided rather than thinking of it as a hovel, it would be my monastic cell. To be a good tenant, I would ask permission to paint and fix it up as I could afford it. Permission was granted, and I soon found myself also freshening up the place with some potted flowers. I watered things from a rainwater barrel that was collecting water from the roof of the apartment. I was as frugal as possible with the electricity. It seemed to me, this solitary life of thrift had much to recommend it. At least for now. It certainly was instrumental in decluttering from my mind the baggage of failure that had come to define me for too long. One day, I suspected I would revisit those years of failure when I could more objectively look backward to sort through the good and the bad. For now, their importance to my present was, thankfully, nonexistent. A proper reexamination of my life would be better done when I had something else to compare it with. Clearly, my life here was going to be a different narrative and thus far a promising one.

While friendly with the people at work and at the food pantry, I wasn't making friends. It wasn't a failure of the community. I was intentionally keeping some distance. From time to time one or another at the food pantry would invite me to go to lunch with them after distribution, but I would always politely decline. I knew this might lead to them stopping altogether, which I might regret, but I was willing to risk it for now. I was still eating all my meals at home or what sack lunch I took with me to work. I had not eaten a single meal out since leaving California. There were several restaurants in town despite the small size of the place, in part I supposed as a result of the tourism traffic the area generated. It would be easy to find a favorite and in so doing part with too much of my meager income. Better to live without the temptation for now.

The old Ranger wasn't going to run forever and when she'd finally die I wasn't going to get any trade-in value or a good loan rate with my credit rating. I figured I could get a loan on another used vehicle when the time came for me to chug her last few miles into a dealership, but that meant another monthly expense I needed to prepare for. For now, my driving was so minimal I had some hope it could last a year or two more—maybe even longer. I'd at least taken fair care of her all the years I owned her so she might survive a while longer than most.

My landlord, coworker and now driver to work always had the radio on. It drove me a little crazy. Chuy would talk like I was supposed to hear what he was saying with commercials and the mariachi brass blaring. Once when a quieter classical guitar piece came on I commented how beautiful I thought it was. He asked if I played the guitar, and I said I did not though perhaps sometime I would buy a guitar and see if I could learn. He didn't say any more about it, but when we got home that evening he went in the house and was back in a moment at my door.

"Here," he said. "This just sits in the case. I thought I'd take it up and never did. You might as well see if you can pick it up or decide if it's too hard. In the case there is a book on basic chords and a few simple songs."

"Thank you, Chuy," I said. "I look forward to trying it out."

I didn't waste any time pulling it out. With no TV, I was certain it would help pass the time and would be a break from reading, which had become my primary pastime. It was close enough to being in tune that I could guess, which strings needed a little fine tuning to sound right with the others. The book was a guitar for beginners, which was a good thing since I not only had never played the guitar, I'd never read music either. I was completely illiterate, though the narrative on how to hold the instrument seemed pretty silly to me. You'd have to be pretty blind to the world around you not to at least know that. I found myself skipping to the first chords and following the diagrams. *brummmm*...I ran the pick across the strings.

It was a nice evening, and I wanted to sit outside in my lawn chair but certainly wasn't ready to serenade the neighborhood. I put the guitar back in the case, got a glass of ice tea and stared at those mountains. I thought about the story in Merton's book of the old monk who asked the young monks what this or that scripture meant. When the last one answered, "I know not," the old monk said he was the only one to answer correctly. I realized how much that aligned with my own understanding of my life.

Chapter Four

I'd had the guitar Chuy loaned me for a couple months. Every evening I would work on learning the chords and was beginning to try to pluck out a couple songs. I'd heard a local cowboy musician play and sing "Annie Laurie," and I was eager to learn it. I found the sheet music in Alpine and got to work on it. I'd never really tried to sing, but I found the ballad something I could at least mumble along as I practiced the guitar. I guess I sounded better than I thought. I'd finally braved sitting outside practicing one evening and Chuy and Lupe were standing at their back door listening, unbeknownst to me.

When I finished the last verse and went silent Chuy said, "Your playing is coming right along. You didn't tell us you could sing."

"Can I?" I asked in all seriousness. "You're probably just being nice. If I can sing, it's news to me, too. I just love the melody too much not to try to sing along."

Lupe said, "You have a very nice voice. You should just sing a little louder."

"Well, maybe tomorrow night. It's getting dark now. I guess I'll be going in."

On the drive to work the next morning Chuy said, "If you keep practicing you could get some work off and on performing around here. I'm not sure that offers any great job security. It appears to me most of the ones doing it are in it only for the joy they get from it. But you might earn a little extra *dinero*."

"I'm not ready to take my act on the road, that's for sure," I said. "I'm pretty sure what playing and singing I'll do will be for my own enjoyment, and if a couple of nice neighbors want to listen in from time to time—well, that would be okay. I won't charge 'em."

That was the end of that as Chuy cranked up the radio during a commercial where the man talked so fast even my mostly bilingual self was left wondering what the hell he was selling. I just had to ask. Much louder than I am ever known to talk I asked, "Can you tell me what he was selling?"

Chuy responded matter-of-factly, "I wasn't listening."

14

Some people prefer noise over any thought that might pass through in the silence if nurtured for any length. Chuy seemed to be one of those people. I just stared out the side window looking at the giant greenhouse we would labor in for another day.

One evening when the three of us were sitting out in the yard with little to say and nothing on our minds in particular, I decided to inquire about a local cowboy I had noticed several times at the grocery store.

"I often see an old cowboy in the Thriftway, who one time looks like he just came in from branding cattle after a long ten-hour day, and who the next time is in a crisp, starched shirt and jeans—so stiff it looks like he couldn't bend his elbows or knees if he tried. On those occasions he has on his bright Tom Mix hat; while, on what I'll call his branding days, it's a hat so old and worn I'm not sure what keeps the brim from falling off from the worn patches all around his headband. He's thin as a rail and tall enough, it looks like all he'd have to do is fling his right leg up high to get on his horse. And he has a staple diet, it appears to me, of Hostess Twinkies and King Edward cigars."

Chuy said, "That would be Bill Schlatter. He married into one of the ranching families out here, the Geermanns, and now runs the bit of that ranch his wife inherited when the original ranch was first split up between the two daughters, Sallie Faye and Betsy-Mae. Bill married Betsy-Mae. They still ranch a fair chunk of grass—I think about fifteen thousand acres. Might be less than that—might be more. Short of gettin' a copy of a survey, there ain't many ranchers gonna tell you how many acres they got or head of cattle unless they just like to brag about it, which most out here don't."

"That's true enough," Lupe said. "That Schlatter woman—now she's interesting. She is real religious and maybe Bill is but don't show it much. She speaks in tongues they say and only has two colors when it comes to any subject—black and white. It hasn't made for much luck with their kids.

"One's a lesbian she never talks to even though she lives in Marfa with her partner and goes to church every Sunday. Another is straight enough. Apparently too much so as he's been divorced more times and with more women than most bucks mate with in a lifetime. And the third took off when he was sixteen, and as far as I know, never was heard from again. I know he didn't come home for any of his grandparents' funerals, and whether he will do so for his parents' remains to be seen."

Chuy interjected, "The only thing I would add to that telling is to say that as Lupe laid out the order of the kids, she took them in reverse order. It's the oldest that took off."

I said, "Out here, I'm a little surprised the daughter and her partner would be open about their relationship."

Lupe said, "It wouldn't do much good to pretend otherwise. In these small communities it would be pretty hard not to see."

And Chuy added, "It must be said, we're a pretty live-and-let-live bunch. With all the oddballs around here, you'd be pretty lonely if you didn't get along with all types."

Then he added, "I have it from a fairly reliable source that Bill Jr., Billy, that one that ran off, does keep in touch with his dad and has made it pretty clear that if his *mamá* ever lightens up, he'd be open to patchin' things up.

"Billy never even got too far from home. He got a job as a ranch hand on a big ranch up somewhere around Van Horn. The ranch has since been bought by one of the mega-rich. Billy's doing pretty well for himself. If Betsy wants to keep that ranch in the family, she'd better ease up since Billy'd be the one to keep the ranch going."

"You never told me any of that," Lupe said.

"That whole situation sounds pretty sad," I said. "What's the point of her being so holy if her own kids don't know what love looks like from their own mother?"

"I don't know the woman," Lupe said, "but I know the woman who goes to her house every week to do housekeeping. She always has one of those TV evangelists on the whole time my friend is there cleaning, and the Schlatter woman only speaks to her when she's got something to say about what she wants done or not done."

Chuy, reflecting on the good that can come about as one ages, added, "Could be she'll see her god is pretty small one of these days, and she'll realize how much she sacrificed out of some idea of her own religion.

"I'm not sayin' we got it all figured out, but—as best I can tell,—if you can't find enough grace for the closest around you, you ain't likely to pass it on to anyone, anywhere, anytime. You've boxed yourself into being 'right' over all else."

"I didn't know you were that wise, my friend!" I said.

Lupe said, "He isn't, but he gets lucky once in a while."

Chuy said, "Well, whatever Betsy-Mae is, Bill is the salt of the earth. He ain't got a pretentious bone in his body. And I have little doubt he'd rather be out on that saddle o' his than sittin' home with that wife o' his. Could be he eats all those Twinkies and smokes those King Edwards to make sure he checks out of life when his ridin' days are o'er rather than risk being cooped up with her in that house in town where she spends all her time."

I said, "While I've never spoken to Bill in the store, he always tips his hat and says, 'Howdy.' He's got one of those faces worn by the sun and the wind—full of dignity and wearing a wry smile."

"I'd say that's pretty accurate," Chuy said. "I don't think there's a soul in town who could find a bad thing to say about Bill Schlatter, while plenty steer clear of Betsy-Mae."

Then he chuckled and added, "He did get a mighty fine ranch out of that marriage. I guess he figures you take the bad with the good."

Lupe said, "She does have her Bible study group she's tight with. They're a mix of bossy women with hen-pecked husbands, wives of husbands who want mousy, obedient wives—which includes their preacher's wife as their role model—and the few odd ducks like Betsy-Mae whose husbands live their lives and let their wives live theirs."

Chuy agreed and added, "That last bunch are mostly ranchers and cowboys. You ain't gonna fence 'em in. Them boys ain't gonna be fenced in no matter how holy their wives think they are."

I picked up my guitar and started to play and sing that old cowboy song I had just learned.

Oh, give me land, lots of land under starry skies above.
Don't fence me in.
Let me ride through the wide open country that I love.
Don't fence me in.

Let me be by myself in the evenin' breeze,
And listen to the murmur of the cottonwood trees.
Send me off forever but I ask you please.
Don't fence me in.

Just turn me loose, let me straddle my old saddle
Underneath the western skies.
On my Cayuse, let me wander over yonder
Till I see the mountains rise.
I want to ride to the ridge where the west commences,
And gaze at the moon till I lose my senses,
I can't look at hovels and I can't stand fences.
Don't fence me in.

I laid the guitar on my lap and said, "Well, that's all I know of that one." I couldn't know it then, but one day my fate and the rancher's fate would intertwine.

Chapter Five

Chuy and I had not yet talked much about his family. I didn't know anything about his parents and thus far we'd only really talked about his youngest brother, Ernesto. You can't live in Fort Davis and not talk about Ernesto. I guess Chuy figured I might just as well hear about his baby brother from him first.

One evening when we'd had supper together, Chuy offered me a beer afterwards, which I thanked him for. Then he started in. "My kid brother is just a little too fond of a Bud six-pack," he said.

Lupe interjected, "If you're starting in on tellin' him about Ernesto, I'm going to do the dishes." Then to me she said, "I hope you're not in a hurry to get back to your room. This could take a while."

Chuy continued with his introduction to his youngest sibling. "*Papá* never spoiled him, but *Mamá* couldn't help herself. Ernesto was born on Christmas Day and so she took it as a sign, 'Oh, this youngest son of mine will be a priest—a vicar for Christ!' She always wanted one of her sons to become a priest. None of us ever did. She drug him to every Mass possible and had him serving as an altar boy as soon as the priest would allow it.

"He never out-and-out rebelled, but it never really took, either. He learned every cuss word pretty early on and had to work like hell not to use one or more in every sentence when he was around *Mamá* like he did the rest of the time.

"Up until she died, he pretty much went to Mass every Sunday. Since then he might show up maybe once a month."

Lupe hollered from the kitchen, "You'd better tell him about New Year's Eve."

"I'm gettin' there," Chuy answered. "Every New Year's Eve his family hosts the Cardonas and he dresses as a drag queen. He even did it when *Mamá* and *Papá* were still livin'. His look the last few years has been to try to look like Rosalind Russell. His wife, Rosalinda, says he looks a lot more like Margaret Hamilton—you know, the wicked witch of the West. He does have the nose for it.

"Anyway, he's been Mae West, Kate Smith and tried one year to look like Sophia Loren. Rosalinda said, 'As Sophia Loren, you leave a lot to be desired.' Whenever he is Kate Smith, he sings "God Bless America" when midnight comes. He never has retired her altogether. One year he told me he was going to dress as the Madonna. *Mamá* was still livin' and I said, 'It'd better be Madonna the singer and not *the* Madonna, or you'll put your twice-a-day, rosary-praying *Mamá* in the grave. It was *the* Madonna he had in mind and decided I was probably right.

"Rosalinda says, 'I think I married a gay man.' Other than his New Year's Eve drag act, there's no indication of that. He loves his wife, his kids, his Bud and his cussin'. I can't see he has any attraction to those of the same sex."

"What a character," I said. "I can't wait to meet him sometime."

Lupe, back from doing the dishes said, "He's entertaining, I'll give him that! You can't help but be amused by him and I swear, no one is more amused by him than he is himself."

I asked, "What does he do for a living?"

Chuy answered, "He does rock and adobe work and has help with carpentry on bigger jobs. If you see a tight-laid river rock wall in town, he probably laid it. A six-pack of Bud doesn't seem to make any difference to his gift for laying up a perfect rock wall or chimney. He is truly gifted in that regard."

Whenever there was a Cardona or Rodriquez family get-together (Lupe was a Rodriquez), it was usually at one of the other siblings' homes, since they all had children and grandchildren while Chuy and Lupe never had any kids. But the first Easter I was there they had invited both sides of the family over for an Easter egg hunt for the children, and I learned this was their one annual hosted family event.

As soon as church was out, the masses descended. I'm not sure what they do if the weather is bad, but since it rarely is in Fort Davis, this year and probably most years, being outside at Easter was as pleasant as it gets. Chuy is a good egg hider. The thing that surprised me was the effort Lupe and her mother, Elma, had gone to the preceding day to make decorated, colored eggs. Dozens of them! Way too many for an egg hunt of even a large family gathering, it seemed to me. Nowhere in sight were any of those cheap Dollar General candy-filled plastic eggs at this egg hunt—

though the kids probably would have preferred candy over a hard-boiled egg.   I respected that tradition hadn't given way to "progress" with sugar-powered eggs the kids, nor their mostly overweight parents didn't need.

As they prepared for this event, I sat in Lupe's kitchen watching the rhythm perfected over years between the two of them.   Little was said as each went about their task. Using red and yellow onion skins, cochineal, flower petals, and sprigs of this and that, they made beautiful, miniature works of art.   They labored on it for hours, and I just watched with both amazement and appreciation—having the good sense not to offer my incompetence where they would feel like they had to work me in somehow knowing such would only be cumbersome for them. One could see what a bond of love this was for the two women and how it had been cultivated with great respect and care over the years. So I sat mostly silent, only helping to dump the large pots of hot water, which they asked me to do for them.

As Lupe said, "You can do Chuy's job. You're obviously far more patient. I always have to go round him up, and he fusses at us about our egg dying."

I was invited to join them for Easter dinner and had the good sense to accept. I expected a big spread of food. Actually, it was pretty simple. Lots of menudo, pork tamales, carne asada, refried beans, guacamole and chips. A bunch of the found easter eggs were quickly turned into deviled eggs by Lupe, Elma and Elma's other daughters.

What else do you need? Well, I needed lots of water. I love a little spice but the tamales and even the guacamole set me on fire. Delicious, but hot! Loving deviled eggs as I do, I tried not to be a hog—and they did cool off the bite of those tamales. But then I'd have to take another bite and set myself on fire again. The tamales outlasted the eggs on my plate.

Eggs are one of those funny things that doctors and governments can't make up their mind on. For a while they are bad and then they're nutritionally rich and shouldn't be feared.   Best I can tell, even people who cut down their egg consumption during the "egg-bad" period never gave up a deviled egg when they're set out. They disappear in a flash. Thus it was, I confined myself this time to two halves though I could have eaten half a plate of them. The Cardona-Rodriquez clan seemed to like them every bit as much as I, and the wisdom of forgoing plastic, candy-filled eggs was on full display as even the younger ones were encouraged to have an egg. I noticed the only thing several of the men ate was a big bowl of menudo and they would drop the eggs right into the soup. Once the eggs ran out, the second bowl of menudo was topped with a tamale.

My introverted self wanted to be sure that at this Easter get-together I met Ernesto. I didn't have to ask which one he was. It became clear within about two minutes of their arrival.

After we ate, I introduced myself and said, "Your big brother tells me your *mamá* wanted you to be a priest. You were her last chance. I guess it wasn't meant to be."

Ernesto said, "If he told you that, I bet that's not all he told you."

"He mentioned something about New Year's Eve traditions," I said.

"Hell, somebody's gotta liven up this bunch o' sorry-asses." He was as amused by his own response as I was.

I couldn't help but notice that he enjoyed about three to four beers to my one. I expected him to be stumbling around before the night was over, but he never really did.

This was my first real experience with a family in a long time. I've been so estranged from my own, I hadn't seen any of them in several years. Even before that, we were a small, odd mix of misfits who barely spoke to each other. What talk was done was usually snarky and condescending towards someone. Maybe you were there when they were talking about you and maybe you weren't. It didn't really matter. Somewhere along the line, it never sank in that to be kind was preferred over being shit-asses. My family had an abundance of those, and as my life started going down-hill the last thing I wanted was to be around people so cynical they could only see the bad in someone. It wouldn't be a stretch to say this Cardona-Rodriquez get-together was the first real family—as it ought to be—that I'd ever seen other than on TV or in the movies. It bore nothing remotely similar to my own experience, and I was deeply moved even as they all laughed and teased each other.

Certainly, no one was in a hurry to leave the Easter gathering. As evening began to roll around, the Cardona boys pulled out their instruments. I had no idea Chuy played the trumpet, but within minutes we had the lively Cardona mariachi band filling the air with their spirited tunes and everyone dancing, clapping, whooping and hollering along. Ernesto joined the band to sing some rousing Mexican folk songs I'd never heard and even did a couple slower love songs. He has an incredible voice. I thought how much his mother would have loved to hear that voice chant the Mass.

With all the lively music filling the neighborhood, I noticed that instead of being annoyed the neighbors began showing up with their own reinforcements of food for the evening grazing that would go on late into the night. Easter is a feast day, and they made the most of it.

I asked Chuy the next day on our way to work, "So does the band come out every year and the neighbors show up to join in?"

"Every year," he said. "You're not used to such a commotion or crowd, are you?"

"No," I said. "But I thought it was wonderful!" Then I added, "Most of Lupe's beautiful eggs were pretty quickly sacrificed for those delicious deviled eggs."

Chuy said, "I tell her every year, 'Just drop 'em in color and be done with it.' She'll have nothing of it. After Elma is gone, Lupe will see it as her calling to carry on what her *hermanas* won't—egg decorating being one of those things and quilting another. She at least gets her sisters to help peel and make the deviled eggs. They all know Elma's recipe and make them for every family get-together."

"I've learned two things now about your wife I didn't know before—she is a true artisan of decorated eggs and a quilter," I said. "I've not seen any quilts when I've been in the house. Does she just do one once in a while?"

Chuy responded, "Oh, no! She's got one going in the back room all the time. They don't stay around long. Anytime there is a niece or nephew born or any new kid at the church, she's there giving a quilt for them. Practically every kid in this town born since we've been married has one of her quilts. I'm not sure what she'd do if someone had triplets. She'd have to get busy quick. As it is, the most inventory she carries is two—as she has needed two for twins on half a dozen occasions over the years."

I said, "That's wonderful. I hope the kids in town appreciate her hard work."

"Most do," he said. "There are a couple families that just take them as though it's their due and never bother to even say 'thank you.' It doesn't matter, she'll do one for their next child—grateful parents or not."

I said, "I ran across an old Latin chant that says 'Where true love and charity are, God is there.' I'd say those are woven into every quilt she makes."

Chuy said, "I'm amazed that every quilt is so different. And she doesn't just whip them together. She makes tiny little stitches. She said to me once, 'Here, sit and make a few stitches. It won't kill you.' So I did and after about two minutes she said, 'Go work in the yard.' That was all she said. I know she pulled right back out the few stitches I put in, but she never said."

We both chuckled at that, and our conversation was up for the time being as we both got out of the truck to start the day's work at the tomato farm.

Chapter Six

Once I made the connection with Ernesto, I realized I'd met his wife numerous times without knowing it. Rosalinda was a regular volunteer at the food pantry. I would learn she was not just a show-up-when-you-feel-like-it volunteer like me, but was there every Friday when the food bank truck came in and every Saturday when the families showed up to get food. She was a real worker. Quiet, compared to Ernesto, but that's not saying much. She's one of those persons you can tell are just really comfortable in their own skin and would not be easily intimidated. I guess you'd have to be that to be married to Ernesto.

After the big Easter get-together, I was at the pantry for every distribution unless I had to work at the tomato farm. I was slowly working my life into the lives of the Cardonas.

To my surprise, one Saturday after distribution Rosalinda said, "Ernesto is meeting me at the Slo Poke Cafe for lunch. Why don't you join us? He said he enjoyed visiting with you at Easter. I told him you're always at the food pantry helping out."

By now, I could afford to eat out if I wanted to, and I was feeling comfortable enough socially to get out more. I said, "Sure, I'd like that."

When we pulled into the Slo Poke Cafe parking lot, Ernesto was sitting in his truck, window down, radio on. Loud radios run in the family it would seem. The cafe was just opening when we got there. Not surprisingly, Ernesto and Rosalinda were clearly well known by the waitress who didn't have to ask what they wanted to drink. She just arrived with two ice teas and asked what I wanted.

It was pretty clear I was supposed to sit next to Rosalinda. Ernesto headed straight for a booth, sat down, slid in to put his back against the wall and legs up on the bench—his cowboy boots hanging off the end. Rosalinda slid in on the other side and said to me, "He likes to make himself at home."

He popped back up long enough to go hang his cowboy hat on the hat rack near the entrance, sat back down and said, "I almost forgot to be a gentleman."

Rosalinda said to me, meaning for him to hear of course, "Thirty years he's been almost forgettin'. I'm not too shy to remind him. That cowboy hat is the least of it!"

Ernesto said, "I can't get this woman to open the damn door for me even if I go to Mass. She'll stand there as though she can't do it just to make me do it for her."

Rosalinda added, "It doesn't take much to entertain us."

We all three ordered the combination fajitas, and then the real purpose of the invitation was made clear. Ernesto said, "I asked Chuy what your story was. He said you don't have much to say other than you came pretty broke from California. You on the run from the law?"

I was pretty sure Chuy and Lupe were very curious about my past but didn't want to pry. The more forthright Ernesto and Rosalinda had no such qualms. It was pretty clear both were curious to know more.

"No, I'm not on the run from the law. I was mostly on the run from myself," I said. "I tried to leave the loser back there and find a fresh start here, which I have to say has brought the first glimmer of hope I've had in a long time.

"I'm not trying to be mysterious about myself or tight-lipped. I had a lot to work through, a lot of years in my mind, and I wouldn't have quite known where to start if Chuy and Lupe had asked. Since you did, I'll give you some of the first pieces of it. It was the Easter get-together that really cracked the first bit of it open where I felt like I began to make some sense of it.

"I've been estranged from my family for so long, I'd begun to think all families were that way. When I saw your families and neighbors having such a great time, I realized that was something I had never seen except as Hollywood fantasy. If you want to know how many of my family have noticed I've left California, my guess would be zero.

"If you want to know if I hope we have some great family reconciliation, I'd just say, 'If I never see any of them again that would be fine by me.' Pretty harsh, huh?"

Rosalinda said, "Must be for good reason."

I continued, "They are just cruel. I don't know why. They can't find a kind word for anyone for any reason. It wears one out. It certainly sent anyone I was ever interested in romantically heading for the hills. One meeting, and they could see the toxicity and that was the end of that.

"I had a grandmother in Connecticut who left each of her grandchildren $75,000. I'd never even met her, but I found myself with a bit of money so I set up my own business. I knew going in I was taking a big risk with trying to start a business in California with that amount of money, but I did it anyway.

"I was actually doing okay for a while, but one blip in the economy, and I found customers soon forgot I existed. I was depressingly broke, and when I couldn't keep the doors open or even pay rent on my shoe-box apartment anymore, I headed here. I suppose Chuy told you I picked Fort Davis because I watched the movie *Dancer, Texas*."

Ernesto said, "He did tell us that much. Did he tell you I was in that movie? They didn't realize what they had. I could have livened things up for those boys. As it was, we 'Mexicans' were just extras."

I confessed, "I hadn't really thought about that before. You're right. None of the main characters were Hispanic even though 'Dancer' looks pretty hispanic when you look around town. I sure did like that movie."

Rosalinda asked, "Are your parents together?"

"Not by a long shot," I said. "They divorced when I was in second grade and there has never been any indication that either knew the other's first name. My father always referred to my mother as shit-head, and my mother always referred to my father as that sorry-son-of-a-bitch. I guess that gives you as good a glimpse as any of the home life we three kids knew as we were passed back and forth between the two of them. My brother and sister seem intent on passing the toxicity on to the next generation. I am done with it!"

The fajitas arrived, sparing me any need for carrying on further about my family. Both Ernesto and Rosalinda looked at their plate, made the sign of the cross and dug in. I smiled to myself as I thought about Ernesto's mother's faith still clinging to her baby boy —priest or not.

After the twice-monthly food pantry distribution, lunch at the Slo Poke Cafe became a regular event. Ernesto would join us if he wasn't out on a job too far to drive in for lunch, and when he was, one or two of the other volunteers would join us. I'd managed to navigate that fine line of staying as detached as I wanted at first without forever alienating the nice people who had offered early invitations to lunch. I found myself really looking forward to Saturdays. And Sunday evenings, weather permitting, I'd be outside in my lawn chair with my guitar, and Chuy and Lupe would be sitting there listening to me sing and play as we all watched the sun set over the Davis Mountains.

There was a breeze one evening, and just when I was about to put the guitar down, I saw a tumbleweed go rolling down the street. I said, "I guess with that tumbleweed rolling by I should play you my latest tune—"Tumbling Tumbleweed."

See them tumbling down
Pledging their love to the ground!
Lonely, but free, I'll be found
Drifting along with the tumbling tumbleweeds

Cares of the past are behind
Nowhere to go, but I'll find
Just where the trail will wind
Drifting along with the tumblin' tumbleweeds

I know when night has gone
That a new world's born at dawn!
I'll keep rolling along
Deep in my heart is a song
Here on the range I belong
Drifting along with the tumbling tumbleweeds

I know when night has gone
That a new world's born at dawn!
I'll keep rolling along
Deep in my heart is a song
Here on the range I belong

When I finished, I was glad for three things. One, that I'd made it all the way through without messin' anything up. Next, that it was getting dark so they couldn't see how I was getting choked up as the words resonated with me in that moment. And finally, that they went on in and I could sit there and ponder something I hadn't even thought about the whole time I was learning that song. My theme song had changed from "All the Gold in California" to this old cowboy song. A new world born at dawn—here on the range I belong.

Chapter Seven

As best I could tell, about half of Fort Davis went to one or another of the churches every Sunday, and the other half either went rarely, or like me, not at all. I half expected Chuy and Lupe to bring it up sometime but they hadn't. Also if Rosalinda or Ernesto had ever said anything to them about my family, there was no indication such was the case. I finally asked them one Sunday evening if they had. By then they knew I had lunch with Ernesto and Rosalinda on a pretty regular schedule.

"No, they never said anything," Chuy said. "The only thing he ever said to me was, 'I hope you like your tenant. I don't think he'll be lookin' for a new place anytime soon and for sure he ain't gonna be headin' back to California.' I said to him we'd sorta gathered you were glad to be away from there."

So, I laid it out as I had for Ernesto and Rosalinda. Feeling I owed them that little bit more, I also included how completely irreligious we were as a family, and how the first prayer I ever made was in their little casita I now called home.

Lupe said, "I see you read from those books by Merton, who I'd heard our last priest mention in homilies but I've never read. I thought maybe you were Catholic but just didn't go to church."

I said, "I've never even been to a wedding or a funeral in a church. I have, as they say, never darkened their door. I might sometime, but for now, the desert and mountains are feeding me what I seem to need most."

Chuy said, "We've had a couple priests over the years who just about ran me off. Since *Mamá* was still living I didn't dare give it up. The last couple have been pretty good. This one we got now is hard to understand. We don't seem to ever get a priest anymore whose first language is either English or Spanish. Well, they speak English but as it's spoken in Africa or the Philippines. Those places seem to be supplying America with the priests they need these days. Fortunately, we never got into the mess some of the parishes have had to deal with.

"When *Mamá* was still living I asked Ernesto if any priest had ever tried anything with him. I thought maybe that would explain something—though I wasn't sure what or how.

"He said, 'Hell no! If he had I'da kicked him in the *cojones*. I wear those outfits to get at *Mamá*.' When he told her there was no damn way he was ever gonna be a priest she said to him, 'I might as well have had another daughter than to have a cussin' boy like you.' 'Oh, you love me *Mamá*,' he said, and she said, 'Yes I do and I don't know why!' That was on his Christmas birthday, and so when she came to the door that New Year's Eve, he was there in a dress for her. She took her purse and hit him with it without saying a word. He's been doing it ever since.

"That's my brother," Chuy said. "Though honestly, there was something about his and *Mamá*'s relationship that none of the rest of us had. I couldn't prove it, but I think *Mamá* looked forward to seeing what he had in store for the family every New Year's Eve. I know it always started with her hittin' him with that purse and then smilin'. *Papá* would just shake his head, look at Ernesto and say, 'The *hija* I never had.' Of course, he had daughters but never one quite like Ernesto."

"Speaking of church," I said, "you told me about Betsy Schlatter but nothing of her sister. You mentioned they both inherited ranch land. Is she around here?"

"Oh, yea," Chuy said. "She almost never comes into town. She's all cowgirl—rides with the ranch hands and leaves all the housework and cooking to a live-in woman who's been with her for years. She's quite a contrast to her straight-and-narrow sister. The only person around who can keep up with Ernesto on cussin' would be Sallie. She smokes those Swisher Sweet Tip Cigarillos, but won't touch a drop of alcohol—at least so far as anyone seems to know about. She's never married. These days, the only church service she ever goes to is Christmas Eve at the Methodist church."

Lupe said, "She and I were in class together growing up. Of course, we all called her a tomboy, which didn't bother her a bit. In fact, I think she preferred it over bein' mistaken for a lady."

Chuy added, "I think if Billy had asked his aunt for a job when he took off from home, she'd have given him one. I always wondered why he didn't go there first."

Lupe said, "He probably didn't want to be any place his *mamá* could figure out easily where he was."

"I suppose that's part of it," Chuy agreed. "You have to remember too that Betsy and Sallie's folks were still living, though barely so, and they were there on the ranch with Sallie. I'm sure Billy didn't want to get in a tangle between his grandparents and his *mamá*. The parents were Church of Christ, and pretty much kept to themselves. I don't know what they thought of how different the two girls turned out. I do know old man Geermann said to me once, 'I lucked into a mighty-fine son-in-law,' and I said, 'Yes, sir, you sure did.'"

Lupe filled in the next couple details. "The old man rode to his last day. His horse stumbled just the least little bit when he was out on a ridge riding with Sallie and a couple of other ranch hands. He lost his balance on that almost thirty-year-old horse of his and went into a gulley and onto a rock. That was the end of him. His wife didn't live two weeks after that and the horse was dead within a month. They all went pretty much together."

Chuy said, "All three are buried out on that ridge where he went down. Betsy wanted to bury them in town, but somehow Sallie got her way on that. Sallie let Betsy have her way on having a service in town, but then both times they loaded the casket in the back of Sallie's pick-up and carried them to their place on the ridge. All the Geermanns up until then had been buried in the cemetery out east. Sallie made it clear she's to be put on the ridge as well."

"I think I'd like Sallie," I said. "She sounds quite formidable."

Chuy replied, "If you see a woman in the Thriftway wearing bib-overalls, that's Sallie. She only comes to town about once a month. She's friendly enough.

"I wouldn't be surprised if she leaves her ranch to Billy, figuring Betsy's gonna force theirs sold since trying to divide it three ways is hard to work out. Certainly, none of them could afford to buy out the other. If Betsy and Bill's ranch does go to all three, they'd be smart to let Billy manage it. I guess only time will tell. That's probably a ways off. Bill's got another good twenty years on that latest horse of his, and God don't want Betsy anytime soon."

With that we all had a good laugh. Just then Ernesto went driving by in his pick-up, window down, arm banging on the door.

"Hey, *caca* head!" hollering for all the world to hear as he drew out the word head.

"Hey, *pendejo*," Chuy hollered back.

"You don't have to encourage him," Lupe said.

"Brotherly love," I added.

Chuy summed it up nicely, "You have to love him."

The next time I was at the Slo Poke Cafe with Ernesto and Rosalinda, and none of the other food pantry volunteers were with us, I got an answer to something I'd wondered about for a long time. Ernesto brought up the topic without me asking.

He asked, "Is my brother going to adopt you? You know they never could have children of their own. Could be they want you for the tax deduction."

"I think I'm a little past the deductible stage," I said.

I didn't want to pry, but I did want to know more about their situation. I said, "No, I didn't know they couldn't. I didn't know whether they didn't want kids or couldn't have kids."

Ernesto continued, "They tried, but also took it as it came. Neither one of them ever went to the doctor to see what the problem might be. Lupe said, 'If it doesn't happen, it doesn't happen. The world will go on and Fort Davis will survive if we don't increase the population.' Chuy said, 'It's not like we need them for company. You and I are pretty happy together.' So they just carried on as though it didn't matter. They each told their folks, 'Don't ask us about grandkids. We're just fine being *tío y tía*.'"

Rosalinda said, "They're as good as gold in that department. Lupe's never been much for baby sittin', but they never forget a birthday, and when the kids are old enough for a bike, they get a brand new one from the two of them. If one of us is sick, she's there with enough food that no one has to cook for a week. I guess you know about her quilts."

"Yes, I do," I said. "Just amazing."

"Ernesto said, "I bet some of those at church who never say thank you probably put them on eBay for a big price."

"Oh, surely not," Rosalinda said.

"I would hope not," I added. "That would be pretty sorry."

Rosalinda thought a moment and said, "If word ever got back to Lupe that they had done that, she'd just say, 'I gave it to them. What they do with it is theirs to decide.'"

I said, "It's kinda like what you said to that new volunteer who thought that young couple at the food pantry snuck out with an extra bag, and she wanted someone to go get it back."

"What'd I say?" she asked. "I don't remember that."

I replied, "It was one of the first times I was there. You said to her, 'If they can live with it, we can live without it.'"

"Well, that's right," she said very matter-of-factly.

Chapter Eight

When you grow up being shuffled back and forth between non-nurturing parents, one eats a lot of fast food. We rarely sat down at a table to eat unless in a fast food restaurant—the dining tables at home merely a shelf for piling anything that didn't get properly put away or disposed of. At my father's, it was mostly old magazines and a few newspapers—even old junk mail he just tossed on the table. At my mother's it was usually unfolded laundry. If we wanted socks and underwear handy in our room, we were expected to go through the pile on the table and do for ourselves. In time, I just found it all easier to do my own laundry. At least, I would take the effort to pull things out of the dryer as they dried rather than leave them to come out a wrinkly mess. We spent slightly more time at her house than at our father's, so we mostly hauled dirty laundry from his to hers.

Once I was on my own, I did upgrade my eating habits somewhat. I certainly wasn't taught to cook growing up, and I didn't make much of an effort to learn once independent. I still ate some fast food but was more inclined to a sit-down meal with proper wait staff. Being a creature of habit, I mostly ate at three different restaurants. All basic diner fare. What I never quite understood was the help. I certainly recognized all the people working there and even could define some of their proclivities. When I saw certain patrons come in, I could guess what they were going to order.

Yet, all the servers (who did come and go, it must be said) couldn't seem to remember any preferences that I might have or regular routine of my ordering. Every day was a new day to them apparently. I would sometimes think to myself, are these Californians dumb or just that self-absorbed? Or am I just in some *Twilight Zone* episode repeating like *Groundhog Day*? I was never sure which of those was closest to reality. It wasn't like they were short of help, either. It always seemed to me like management would do well to hire quality over quantity.

It didn't take many visits to the Slo Poke Cafe before I decided they had done exactly that. While I only went on Saturdays a couple times a month, I quickly saw that Sara, the only waitress in the place, has a mind like a steel trap. She knows all the locals' names, which didn't surprise me too much, but she also knows every preference and quirk they might have. The menu is a large mix of Tex-Mex and American fare and there are no warnings of "no substitutions" on this menu. I've heard numerous "regulars" to the Slo Poke Cafe come up with their own creative combination of what it is they are in the mood for.

Sara takes it all in without writing down a single thing and is back in a while with exactly the order as requested. Some, she doesn't even have to take their order. One elderly man is there every Saturday I've ever been there. He always comes in with a book, sits in the same booth if empty and starts to read. Sara comes to his table with one of those little stainless steel tea pots full of steeping tea, a cup and saucer and two slices of lemon. She doesn't ask what he wants and never offers a menu. At first I thought he must just be there for the tea. A few minutes later—every Saturday —she's back with a bean burrito with some chopped lettuce, tomato and grated cheddar.

During busy tourism times, Sara may get the help of someone to bus the tables, but she's a one-woman show as far as taking the orders and bringing out the food. I marvel at her steady, calm pace. It would seem that nothing can get her to break her stride. She even meets you at the register to settle up. A lesser server would be in tears and have orders so screwed up customers might never come back. As I understand from Rosalinda, they have a second competent server to split the days Sara is off. The Slo Poke Cafe is open seven days a week for lunch and dinner. Sara works Saturday through Wednesday lunch, and the other server, Alicia, the balance.

One spring break, a group of post-college-age kids came in—carrying their six-packs since the Slo Poke Cafe is BYOB, and talking loud enough they seemed to think we all wanted to hear them and nothing else. I'm easily annoyed by such mob-rule. Two things were obvious from the start. They came from a little bit too much privilege and pandering back home, and they had plenty of condescension towards anyone serving them.

Ernesto picked up on it immediately just as I had, though he framed it in his own context. As Sara tended to them just as she would her most loyal and well-tipping customers while they extended zero courtesy to her—going so far as to chastise her for not writing down their orders as she took them—Ernesto said, "That Sara—another lazy Mexican."

I guess it was like rubber-necking on the freeway. The three of us just had to sit there longer than usual to see how it all played out. Of course, Sara got all the orders correct and since they were drinking beer, all she really had to do on that score was discard the empties as they piled up. When they finally got up to leave, it looked like about what you'd expect. Huge plates of food ordered and half eaten; chips all over the table and the floor; paper napkins stuffed into water glasses or into their leftover food; paltry tips on the table.

At least the decibel level had finally dropped back to normal.

Rosalinda said, "I feel like I have jet lag. Poor Sara. Look at the mess they made. I just don't understand people like that. How they think they are superior to everyone else when a hog has better manners is beyond me."

All I could say was, "I concur with that."

Ernesto had his more colorful vocabulary to add. "Mothe-"

Before he could get more out, Rosalinda cut him off, "Don't say it!"

I laughed and said, "Could be we all thought it just the same."

"Damn right," Ernesto said, as he mumbled it under his breath anyway.

Sara came to our table after she'd cashed them all out shaking her head. She said, "Charming bunch. I see you stayed for the entertainment."

Rosalinda said, "I speak for all of us. You're a saint."

Sara replied, "You wouldn't say that if you knew what I would have liked to have said to them."

I said, "Unless we want to condemn ourselves for the same thoughts, we'd still have to say you're a saint."

She walked to the kitchen saying for any and all in the restaurant to hear, "I hope they don't come back."

As we got up to leave, all three of us looked at each other with a confirmation of what the best thing to do in the moment was. We each put a twenty down on the table and met Sara at the cash register.

Chapter Nine

After I'd been at the tomato farm for some time—three years to be exact, I took my first couple of days off. I chose a Thursday-Friday so I'd have a long weekend. It wasn't like I had any plan to do much. In fact, since it was a food pantry distribution weekend, I decided to go in Friday morning, help unload the truck and pack the bags for the next day.

Per her routine, Rosalinda was there and a couple other Saturday regulars—the director, Emma, being one of them, of course. Mostly it was new faces. I was quickly introduced and put to work. The time flew by. The process could only be described as efficient and the atmosphere convivial. Afterwards, I stayed to sweep up, and it gave me a chance to talk to Emma about something I'd wanted to ask her about but never had the chance. I'd heard her make a comment to someone once to the effect, "Oh, she and that group are some of the ones who think we shouldn't exist." I was particularly interested in that comment because I thought it was Betsy Schlatter who was being referenced. But I wasn't certain about that.

I started by saying, "You do such a great job with this place, and the families coming in are so appreciative. Tell me about why some people don't think this should exist."

Emma said, "I gather you heard me say something along that line sometime."

"Yes I did," I responded.

"Me and my big mouth," she said chuckling a bit to herself. "I've had women in this town who have said exactly that to me. We're an embarrassment to this community. There's no real poverty here—just people becoming dependent on handouts."

"Really?" I asked. "I don't know how destitute people are, but there are certainly more poor than rich in this county."

She said, "Well, you and most people get that, but there are the few who can't abide charity even though most of them have what they have because of inheritance or some other lucky breaks in life. But we do exist despite them, and there are extremely generous people in this county who make sure the work continues. I'm sure you've heard me say, we are able to distribute the highest per capita food allowance in the state. That is due to the fact that more people support what we do than those campaigning against it. We even have clients who give back both of their time and even a few dollars here and there as a way of showing their gratitude for the security of knowing we are here month after month."

"That's wonderful!" I said. Then I got my nerve up to ask what I'd wanted even though I thought Emma might skirt the question. "Is Ms. Schlatter's Bible group one that supports the work, or are they the mouthpiece for the women's resistance?"

She laughed, "The women's resistance. I like that. To be candid, yes, Betsy has made it quite clear that we are a disservice to the community even though she probably doesn't realize that her husband is a significant donor. She is the main cheerleader for that group when it comes to anything to do with the food pantry. I might feel bad about saying all this about her, but since she keeps it no secret, it's hardly revealing things I shouldn't."

I said, "And she is one of those, as you say, who has what she has because of inheritance."

Emma just shook her head in agreement then added, "Once we built the new building I think she and her group decided we were here to stay with or without her approval. She just ignores me these days."

"She does that with her own children as I understand it," I said.

"And there you have it," Emma said. Then she asked, "Did you want to go have lunch somewhere? My treat."

"You don't have to treat me, but sure, I'd love to go to lunch. It's your pick as to where we go."

She said, "I gather from your outings with the Cardonas that the Slo Poke Cafe is a favorite. That's where I usually go on Fridays."

"Sold!" was all I said.

When Emma and I got to the Slo Poke Cafe, I finally met the Friday help—the other server, Alicia. With almost as much efficiency as Sara, she was there with Emma's ice tea and wanting to know if I needed a menu—knowing Emma would not. I passed on the menu, and we both ordered what we had on our mind before arriving. Without discussing it, we almost ordered the same thing.

Emma said, "I'll have my usual bean chalupa and a guacamole chalupa."

I said, "I'll take ice tea, one of each of those same chalupas plus a beef chalupa."

I noticed Alicia wrote it down as we spelled out our order.

Emma chuckled. "Your beef chalupa order reminds me of a friend in San Antonio. She said to me once, 'Try to explain Tex-Mex to someone. What's a burrito? It's a tortilla with meat and cheese. What's a taco? Tortilla, meat and cheese. What's a chimichanga? Tortilla, meat and cheese. What's a chalupa? Tortilla, meat and cheese. What's a quesadilla? Tortilla, meat and cheese.'"

"She has a point," I said. "Pretty funny."

Before all the Tex-Mex descriptions began, Alicia was off without a word to get it all going in their efficient kitchen. One doesn't see the actual owners very often unless one of them comes to help at the register or even bus tables. I've never seen either one take an order though they will bring out food once in a while. They are a husband and wife team who do all the cooking and, so far as I know, all the dishwashing too except for those peak times when a nephew comes in to help bus tables and do whatever they put him to doing in the kitchen. I've never really "met" either one of them though they recognize me as a somewhat regular—not too regular by their standard of clientele.

Emma had heard that a movie had brought me to Fort Davis—pretty much anyone who knew me in any context knew that much. She wanted to know more about my leaving California, which she didn't know anything about. There is no way to give an honest accounting of that without a dump of the family life I knew.

Most people look rather aghast as I share the details. Emma started smiling and finally said, "At the end, my father was in the hospital for a couple weeks before he died. One day when he wasn't in his room my brother and I went to the nursing station to see where he was. Two of the nurses there said, 'Oh, your father is such a sweet man. How lucky you are to have a father like that.' My brother, Claude, and I looked at each other and thought, 'What

41

man are these people talking about?' Sweet was not a word we'd ever used to describe him."

Clearly, she didn't hold any hatred toward the man. She said, "It amused us greatly that the gruff, disapproving perfectionist would charm the nurses."

I asked her, "Did you grow up in Fort Davis, or how did you end up here?"

Emma said, "No, we did not grow up here and no, we didn't show up after watching a movie, though that act of faith is rather compelling to me in its own way.

"We're old San Antonio natives. Not quite back to the Alamo but shortly thereafter. As a family, we came to both Big Bend National Park and the State Park here at least every other year. It was the one time dear old dad would actually lighten up. That may be why my brother and I like it so much.

"Neither one of us ever had or wanted children. Our spouses weren't so firmly set on that, but we prevailed.

"When my husband died and Claude's wife died soon thereafter, both from cancer, we decided it made sense to live together and downsize—both of us having bigger houses than we needed or wanted as part of our concession to the no children bargain. We figured while we were taking on such a big life-change, we might as well include a big move. That's how we ended up here."

I interjected, "I didn't know your brother was out here. I've not seen him at the food pantry, or if I did I didn't know it."

She explained, "Claude's almost ten years older than me and says he's too old to lug food around for other people. You've probably seen him and don't know it. He's an old man who comes in here every Saturday to read and eat his bean burrito. There is no slower eater on the planet."

I smiled brightly saying, "Ah yes, I see him all the time. I just never asked Ernesto or Rosalinda what they knew about him. I'm not even sure why I didn't think to ask."

"Despite our age difference," she said, "we've always been close —sometimes to the frustration of our mates who felt out in the cold when we would get tickled by something at their expense. Neither of us has been fans of taking life too seriously. Perhaps a logical extension of a father who took everything too seriously and a mother who at home was a rug for him to stomp on—emotionally not physically.   He never hit any of us—I should at least acknowledge that."

Alicia brought our chalupa plates and more ice tea, and Emma continued her story between bites.

"Besides, both my brother and I had serious enough jobs that the last thing we wanted was heavy downers away from work. Claude was a federal defense attorney, forever beating his head against judges and prosecutors who insist the most expeditious outcome is a plea bargain whether the person is innocent or guilty. The system hardly fosters heroic stands for justice.

"I was a parole officer. Can you imagine that? I certainly had some scary clients who I wondered how they ever got out of prison in the first place. Then there was the whole other lot that broke my heart. They were snagged in some nonviolent offense and thrown into the nightmare jails only to come out the other side wounded or soul-lost or in most cases, both.

"Claude and I both knew colleagues, though that is a far too generous term, who for lack of a better description were lazy-ass, indifferent people drawing a paycheck.   They don't help the problem. If they ever had an idealistic notion of a calling to work for justice, they'd lost it and apparently forgot they ever had it."

"What did your parents do that you both ended up working in the justice system?" I asked.

"The injustice system," she said.   "We got a heart for justice from our mother. She didn't have a job as defined by the economy, but she worked every election getting people to register to vote. She'd march in the street for every just cause that came along, and she ran a winter soup kitchen downtown. Claude and I dished up soup plenty of times.

"Dear Dad was less concerned about justice and more about perfection. To his credit he was an accomplished engineer; he just couldn't engineer feelings into his family life. Nor could he stand for anything to be out of place. Fortunately, our mother found a life outside the home—she wasn't going to get any affection or gratitude from Dear Dad."

I said, "One person in our lives to the good can offset all manner of bad influence. And one to the bad can certainly bring a weight upon families that is hard to overcome. Clearly, you, Claude and your mother did overcome the bad."

As we headed to the register to pay, she said, "Yes we did. And now we're here loving Fort Davis."

"Me too," I replied.

Chapter Ten

For my long weekend, I really wanted to drive down to Big Bend, but I just didn't have confidence in the Ranger pickup to get me there and back. I was certain if it died down there, it would be not only lots of trouble but a near financial disaster. So, along with my extra day at the pantry and my outing with Emma, I stuck to in-town activities. I went to tour the Fort, which I had yet not done, and was surprised to learn that the Buffalo Soldiers were among the troops stationed there.

I have to say that it looked to me like being stationed there in the Fort's heyday was a pretty cushy assignment. Nice quarters in a great natural setting with being alert and ready as the main day-to-day chore. The Fort has survived longer as a relic and attraction than as a working fort. It would be nice if that were always the case, I thought to myself, as the guide laid out its history.

Then I took the hike up the mountain and into the state park. What a great view from up there! I stood there several minutes looking out over the vast terrain.

Suddenly, my mind took me to an imaginary encounter with a sophisticated urbanite coming up next to me with a zoned-out look on her face, asking, "What are you looking at? I don't see anything." And I answer her, "Therein lies the problem." She turns to leave. I think—just up here trying to get a cell signal.

Back to reality, I went down the mountain and over to the lodge for lunch and explored what one could of the old adobe structure. Magnificent! The labor of a government program that actually continues to benefit its citizens. Can't beat that.

By the time I got back to my casita, the full moon was rising as the sun was setting. I sat in my lawn chair with a renewed sense of awe for where I found myself. Perhaps renewed is the wrong word. I've never been insensitive to the awe of this place. I'm not sure what the right word is. Renewed, refreshed? My reluctance to settle on either word was the realization that I had a hard time seeing I was ever "new" or "fresh" and thus to be either renewed or refreshed was incongruent with my former life. Now both words were companions on my daily journey in this place. Still amazed I was here at all—being renewed and refreshed with every waking moment! Free from the weight of the shackles my pride had placed upon me. Free at last to be.

I sat there for a time, and I found myself saying out loud as the moon rose in the sky, "You'll sleep good tonight."

And I did. When I woke up Sunday morning, I had my first notion that I might get ready and walk over to the Catholic Church. I knew the Cardonas would give me a ride, but I didn't want to fully commit by asking them. Just as well. The mood left me about as quickly as it had come.

I still had no TV nor felt any need for one. I still had no computer nor felt any need for one. I still had no phone nor felt any need for one. The one technology I had allowed myself was a CD player and small stereo system. I only had three CDs. One of cowboy music, one of Beethoven's *7th Symphony*, which I found, used, at the bookstore in Alpine, and one of Bible stories that Lupe had given me along with a Bible—"if I was ever curious." She warned me the stories were really meant for children and wasn't trying to insult me. I assured her that most children growing up in any church would be way ahead of me.

Merton's books were certainly instructive of the Catholic faith, though as far as enlightening me on the Bible itself I didn't get much from them. I certainly knew he took issue with how Christianity had put much of its work into practice, and I could at least bear some witness to that fact from what I'd seen of churches.

The Bible story CD had its own accompanying book with pictures so kids could follow along, and it showed the book, chapter and verses where the stories came from. Only because I was drawn to the coat of many colors of the Joseph story did I pick that one as the first to listen to. Perhaps that was a mistake. I should have skipped to the New Testament, but I didn't. Because I had no preconceived notions of what it was that I was supposed to hear or read into the story, I was taken aback by reading the text after I'd listened to the story. I was so taken aback I listened to it again and read it again. Then I read it a third time. I really wanted to talk to Lupe about it, but my courage to do so failed me.

As I understood the story, this favorite son, in his coat of many colors, was ill-treated by his brothers so that God could use him to save the people from starvation. His dreams would yield big payoffs for humanity.

Yet when I read the story from start to finish, it seemed to me he was a sell-out—a conniving and opportunistic man. Did he ever get word to his beloved father he was alive and well and employed as top advisor to Pharaoh? Were the people of the land given a heads-up of his vision of seven years of surplus before seven years of famine arrived so everyone could stock up? Even his own "beloved" father—was he told? No, he oversaw the accumulation of surplus—buying grain on the cheap, storing it in expanded facilities built by slaves of the empire. Then when the famine hit, he took the people's money, then their animals, then their land until Pharaoh owned all the land and the people. The ultimate gift to Joseph's own people? Four hundred years of slavery.

Off to a confusing and frustrating start, I decided I was in no rush to explore a second story on a fine Sunday morning. It did make me think that whoever put the story down in the first place at least had enough integrity to lay out the problem alongside the version Joseph and his descendants no doubt favored. History by the victor as they say or perhaps as may be the case. Blindly sanitizing our preferred narrative. Standing alongside the prophet who tries to get us back on the straight and narrow. The latter usually is a near lost cause—confirmed this morning in my mind by the story of *The Coat of Many Colors*.

Chapter Eleven

I had not told anyone that my long weekend happened to coincide with my thirty-fourth birthday. I'm not much for celebrating them anyway, but no one had ever asked, and I had never said when it was. My birthday also more or less coincided with my arrival in Fort Davis three years earlier. Here it was May 2003. It was hard to believe that much time had passed.

Once away from the CD player, having my fill of Joseph, I went for a long walk around town. The Slo Poke Cafe was just opening up as I went by. I waved to Sara but just kept going. I wasn't really hungry and thought maybe I'd stop in later. By the time I strolled home a couple hours later I saw Ernesto's truck there, and was greeted with a loud shout as he saw me saunter down the street, "Where the hell have you been, chico?"

I immediately thought something must be wrong. "What's happened?"

His answer was a relief and a surprise. "You're missing your own damn birthday party. We've been waiting here an hour for you. Lupe said, 'Oh, he never goes anywhere on a Sunday morning.'"

"What makes you think it's my birthday?" I asked.

He answered, "My brother looked it up at work. You're busted!"

"Can't keep anything a secret in this town!" I said back to him.

By now they were all outside including Lupe's mother, Elma. As we went back in the house I saw the big cake, beautifully decorated. Lupe said, "*Mamá* made this cake for you. She said, 'He's such a nice boy.'" To my surprise, Elma actually came over to me to give me a hug. That was all it took. I started to cry.

Of course, Ernesto had to say something to that. "What's all this? Haven't you ever had a birthday party before?"

I said, in all truthfulness, "No. I haven't."

There was a momentary silence, as what they knew to be my truth from my ridiculous family sank in.

The better angels of Ernesto's nature kicked in as he led a rousing *Cumpleaños Feliz* with that beautiful voice of his—followed by cracking a beer open for himself and one for me.

We didn't dig into the cake just yet. Ernesto had brought over *barbacoa* he'd had in his smoker overnight, Elma had made a huge plate of deviled eggs and Lupe had a pot of pinto beans, guacamole and fresh tortillas.

I said the only thing one can say to all that. "Wow!" Then I surprised myself by saying, "If you'd like, I'll offer a slight variation on a Merton blessing."

Elma as elder spoke for the group. "You go right ahead."

They all made the sign of the cross, and I prayed my first public prayer.

Let us taste no food that does not strengthen us to show thy great love and mercy. Amen.

They repeated the amen and again made the sign of the cross. Lupe looked rather peculiarly at me. "That's beautiful," was all she said. Then she hugged me.

I can't think of a day in my life when I've been hugged by two people. Their gesture prompted the others to all do the same.

As we feasted, they wanted to know how I'd spent my long weekend. I shared with them my Friday food pantry experience, lunch with Emma, my trip to the Fort and State Park and finally my stroll around town. I decided to skip my Sunday morning dig into the Old Testament for now.

I asked how church was, and Chuy said, "One of the good things about being Catholic is even if you can't understand the priest, you still know what's going on."

"I gather his English hasn't improved much," I said.

Lupe said, "His English or Chuy's hearing. You can understand him, but you do have to listen carefully. Therein lies the problem."

Rosalinda said, "Chuy at least shows up. Today Ernesto couldn't go, of course, because he had to tend to his *barbacoa*. Next week it will be something else in the smoker that can sit there most of the night unattended but not one hour during Mass."

Ernesto's answer to that was, "It's the natural law of smoking meat. You can't go against nature."

Elma, who had been very close to the two men's *mamá*, had the last word, "Your mother thought you could at least make an effort."

As we feasted, Ernesto and Chuy entertained us with stories of birthdays in the Cardona household. According to Ernesto, one year by the time he got home from six-man football his brothers and sisters had eaten all his birthday cake.

All Chuy would say about it was, "That might have happened."

If Elma hadn't been in the room I'm sure Ernesto would have added a colorful flourish to that near admission, but instead he just said, "See? He can't deny it."

Chuy had to admit that as the oldest he always got new things, while as the family grew, anything that could be handed down went to the next one in line.

Ernesto said, "By the time I got a bike, it looked like it had been sandblasted and the rust left to grow. I got some orange neon paint and gave it a whole new look."

Chuy said, "You had to dim your headlights at night if you came up on that bike—it would blind you otherwise."

The brothers carried on, and we all just listened in delight at the simple memories carried by a family that knew love at its core.

After the feast and celebration had wrapped up, I went back to my little apartment, plopping onto the bed on my back, and stared up at the ceiling. For several minutes I replayed a sentence over and over in my head before I finally said it out loud, though there was no one there to hear it. "Why do I mean *anything* to these people?"

I didn't have a clue. It didn't take any pondering to see why they would mean something to me. With my arrival on their doorstep, I was as a shell of a man with no hope. I thought of the term Emma used for some of her parolees—soul-lost. I thought that was a near approximation of my life three years ago and before, though I couldn't have really acknowledged that I had lost my soul. It was more the case I didn't feel I had a soul.

I reached over to my nightstand to turn on the lamp and picked up *The Wisdom of the Desert* that had travelled with me from

California and had opened my mind to a new reality. I just opened it to a random spot. It fell to page 119. The brother asked one of the elders about humility who answered, "To do good to those who do evil to you." Did that mean I needed to make some effort to reconcile with my family? That wasn't in my mind a thing I needed to do. It went on a bit further when the young brother didn't really like that answer. I didn't either. The young monk asked, "Supposing a man can't go that far, what should he do?" And the old man answered, "Let him get away from them and keep his mouth shut."

I smiled, said my evening prayer of gratitude and added out loud, "Staying away from my family and keeping my mouth shut—I can do that!"

It probably wouldn't seem like it to most people, but the long weekend I'd just had seemed rather extraordinary to me. I had such gratitude for every day of it. As I was putting the book back on the nightstand, it fell off and the paper jacket came off the hardcover book. Underneath, unbeknownst to me, was an excerpt someone had typed up from Robert Weston's *Seasons of the Soul*. I didn't know the book or the author. It spoke of our connectedness to all that is. It was the last line that really hit me.

The folly is that we soon forget.

I knew as I went to sleep that night that I didn't want to fall into such a folly. I would always try to remember—we are connected.

Part II

Chapter Twelve

One Saturday morning when Ernesto knew there were no food pantry duties, he showed up at my door about 9:00.

"I'm driving into Alpine to go to the feed store. Do you want to ride along?" he asked.

I was a little surprised by the invitation but said, "Sure."

As we headed out I asked, "What are you buying feed for? Do you have chickens or something?"

He answered, "We do have some chickens, and I will get them some feed while I'm there. I'm really going to look at tractors. I'd like to get one with a front-end loader and a backhoe both, so when I need one, which is pretty often, I don't have to keep renting one."

That was about all the conversation I was going to get out of him for the time being. Like his older brother, the radio was cranked up for almost the entire drive down to Alpine. He did turn it down when we got to the first sharp turn as we drove into the mountains.

He had a seriousness in his voice I wasn't quite used to. "If you come through here in the winter, you really have to be careful. This is the corner where our *papá* was killed. He was driving back from Alpine and hit black ice. His truck went out of control and rolled and killed him. That was just before you moved here. If Chuy seemed a little quiet back then, that's why. It even had me quiet for while."

A minute of silent contemplation about that memory followed and then the radio was cranked back up. He drove with one arm out the window and sang along in full voice anytime he knew the song, which was most of them.

Between songs and over the too-loud commercials I hollered — or at least I felt like I was hollering — "Your brother doesn't serenade me on the drive to the tomato farm."

"That boy can't sing a note, though he plays a pretty mean mariachi trumpet," he said.

I just shook my head in agreement.

While Alpine is a big town compared to Fort Davis, by city standards it is still barely more than a village. The small, yet impressive, state university sits prominently up on the east side of town perched on the lower side of a mountain. We went past the university to the feed store, which, for a small town, maintains an impressive inventory of John Deere tractors.

The store owner was already outside among the tractors talking with a familiar man—Bill Schlatter. He was there looking for a tractor as well. I was not at all surprised by the charismatic Ernesto's interruption of their conversation. Neither were they— both clearly knowing him well.

After shaking both their hands with great vigor, Ernesto gestured to me, saying to them, "You probably don't know this *hombre*—he's *Jaime* Cruz and lives in my brother's casita. He still goes by Cruz but we've made him mostly a Cardona by now. He came here from California."

Each shook my hand and introduced himself in return, Bill adding, "I've seen you in the Thriftway. Nice to put a name with the face."

Jerry, the owner, noticing Ernesto looking at tractors asked, "Ernesto, you here to buy more than chicken feed today—you gonna buy a tractor?"

Ernesto answered, "Thinkin' about it. I thought if I brought *Jaime* along he might buy it for me."

I said, "On my tomato farm wages it might take me a couple decades to pay it off." I didn't see any point in hiding where I worked or the modest income I lived on.

Bill seemed as curious, or more so than Jerry, as to what it was that Ernesto wanted.

Ernesto said, "I'm looking for something big enough to have a good front-end loader and a decent sized backhoe. Any big rock job and I need a tractor. It would come in handy, too, when I'm making adobe."

Bill really shocked Ernesto with what came next. Making Ernesto speechless is something I'd never witnessed, and I was glad I was there to see it.

53

Bill said, "I have a proposition for you, and I think it's one Jerry won't fuss about either. I'm here to get a little tractor with a bush-hog. I've been wanting to talk to you about doing some work for me. Might be I'll buy you that tractor if you come build me a ranch house out on the ranch.

"You know Betsy never was keen on moving out to the ranch, but she's had a bit of a falling out with her church group and says she's ready to move to the ranch if I'll build her a proper house. I was thinkin' somethin' in adobe and rock, which is why I was thinkin' of you. I just hadn't gotten around to calling you yet. Seems like fate might have taken care of my procrastination for me."

Jerry, seeing that Ernesto was speechless for the first time ever said, "Cat got your tongue, Ernesto?" Then he said to Bill, "I don't mind a bit selling you two tractors, a front-end loader, a backhoe and a bush hog as long as you're not wantin' two for one. I know you'd want two tractors so you aren't holdin' each other up."

I think Jerry was then as surprised as Ernesto when Bill said, "I didn't think you'd give me two for one, but two is what I'd want to buy if Ernesto will come do the work for me. I didn't mention a blade, but I'd wanna buy one of those while I'm at it.

"Ernesto, I'm sure we could work out a fair deal for both of us where at the end that tractor would be yours."

Bill walked over to the largest tractor on the lot, which was already fitted with both the front-end loader and the backhoe.

"Well, boys, what do you think? Jerry, you wanna sell this one? Ernesto, you ready to put it to work? Do you need to think about my offer or do you think we can move forward assuming we'll come to an agreement. We know each other well enough to shake on it, don't we?"

Ernesto did just that. He reached out his hand to shake Bill's. Then getting back to his lighthearted self he turned to Jerry and said, "Looks like all I might be buying today is chicken feed after all."

Bill said, "Jerry, you know what we want. Get it all worked up and give me a call. Ernesto and Jaime, if you got time we'll run out to the ranch now, and I'll lay out what I have in mind. Will that work for you boys?"

Ernesto already knew I didn't have any plans for the day and so he said, "Yes, sir, that will work for us."

Jerry shook all our hands, and we got back in our truck and followed Bill to the ranch.

Ernesto turned off the radio. He said to me, "What the hell just happened!? Are you some good luck charm I didn't know about?"

"Don't know about that," I said. "If I am, it would be something new in my life, that's for sure."

Then he said, "You tired working at that tomato farm yet? My hand told me yesterday he's movin' to Midland. If I get this work from Bill, I'm gonna need help pretty quick."

I said, "I've never driven a tractor or built anything. What good would I be to you?"

"Call it a feeling," he said. "Why did I pick you up this morning? I didn't know myself. I just sorta steered over there and you were home and ready to go. Then we just happened to get to the store when Bill Schlatter is there buying a tractor and planning to talk to me about building him a home. My gut says you're supposed to be part of this."

I commented, "Interesting that Betsy's had a falling-out with her church group. Maybe this will open the door for Billy to come home. Could be she's lightenin' up. We'll see what happens at the ranch in a bit here, but if you're brave enough to hire, I'm probably brave enough to give it a shot."

Ernesto just followed the pickup in front of us. He never did turn the radio back on and neither of us said another word.

Chapter Thirteen

When we first entered the ranch, we passed an old, rather run-down building, which Ernesto explained was the original adobe bunkhouse and still used on occasion for anyone staying overnight during calving season or extended ranch work. Beside it was a large shed wrapped in corrugated steel, several pens and a chute for loading the cattle into semi-trailers. I asked Ernesto where the horses were, and he said Bill kept those over at Sallie's since no one stayed at Bill's full-time.

What those first buildings lacked in tidiness and care, the ranch itself exuded careful stewardship. It was then and remains, perhaps the healthiest stand of grass I've seen in the area—not a mesquite bush in sight. Even a city boy like me can spot care when he sees it, and this place was well cared for. The cattle out on the grass were beautiful, and I had an overwhelming sense that somehow, for our very survival, we needed to learn from that which might be rare but still altogether real—the good stewardship of the best ranchers and farmers.

Radio mercifully still off, I said to Ernesto, "If I had my lawn chair, I could just sit right here and stare at this for a long time."

There never was a proper ranch house on this part of the ranch. That house, of course, was across the other cattle guard where Sallie now lived—where she had lived all those years with her and Betsy's aging parents. On that part of the ranch, too, is where both parents are buried and now, for the first time, the place where it seems likely both their daughters and grandchildren might be laid to rest in the years to come. The simplicity of this notion and the healing that seemed possible now for this family, as it came to me in that moment, nearly brought me to tears. The beauty of the place quickly moved beyond the emotion stirred in that moment and back to something more akin to a giddy excitement.

On this August Saturday, the rains had sweetened the grass to bright green as the grama was still in its peak growth cycle with just a few seed heads starting to appear. The land was flat with a few spots possessing a gentle undulation—and always beyond the plateau in every direction were the mountains. I could see Mount

Livermore with its funny little knob-top as I looked back to the south—if I wasn't all turned around. We seemed to be driving north, which was confirmed when we stopped at a ridge. It only took one look to see why Bill stopped here. We all got out and stared at the expanse of mountains that lie beyond the high ridge of the high plain we had stopped upon in the foot-tall grama. Beyond the mountains you could see the flat desolate counties to north of Jeff Davis. I didn't know for sure, but I suspected on this clear day it was New Mexico off on the horizon.

The first thing Ernesto said was, "I see he's had a well and electric back here for a long time. He's watering from here. I'll bet he's wanted to live on this ridge since he started working here as a ranch hand even before he married into the land."

I said, "I like the way you put that—married into the land."

He replied, "Well, that's what he did, isn't it?"

I felt no need to confirm.

Bill was staring out across the ridge as we approached. Without turning his gaze from it, he said, "I need to say something about my comments regarding my wife that I said when we were in town. I've already called Jerry on my cell phone to be sure I don't get myself in the dog house.

"I said my wife has had a falling out with her church group. The part of that, which might seem a foregone conclusion would be that they are aware of such a falling out, which they are not. She has had what she calls her epiphany.

"At the last Texas Cattlewoman's meeting, a Marfa woman, who goes to the Episcopal Church where our daughter and her partner go, gave my wife a book. She's our age but has long befriended the girls. She's never said anything to Betsy at any other meetings about them or if she runs into Betsy in one town or the other. I know Betsy has seen the three of them having lunch together in Alpine every now and again.

"Well, she read it, and then she read it a second time. She didn't say anything the first time through, and since she's always reading religious books and nothing else, I didn't think anything was going on out of the ordinary.

"Once through the second time she said to me, 'I should have been reading books like this all these years instead of the junk our ladies' group reads.' What do you mean by that? I asked. And she said, 'I would have known how to love my children.'

"With that she handed me the book and asked me to read it. I'm not the reader she is, but I read it. It's by a man in Nashville— name of Benson. It's called *The Body Broken* in case you're interested. When I got through it, it confirmed what I've long held more as my religion, which never fit with hers.

"Anyway, I'm getting mighty long-winded for me. She just hasn't figured out what she's gonna do about church, but she knows she wants to move past their doctrine of certainly and entertain pondering for a change. She said, 'The miles between church and the ranch might do me good.' She didn't have to ask me twice, that's for sure. I've wanted to come out here since I was eighteen when we first got engaged."

Then he shifted gears, "Let's talk house. I asked a couple people who have used architects about how much money they had to sink into hiring one and what they thought they got out of it. They seemed okay with the work but for the price of a John Deere the fees seemed pretty steep to me. I'm hoping we can put our heads together and come up with our own plans."

Ernesto offered him some reassurance. "I don't need much more than a floor plan and some agreement on the type of roof, where you want rock and how much wood you wanna use."

"That's what I was hopin'," Bill said. "Betsy doesn't have any vision for such things, and I don't have much more, but I figure this ridge defines a lot of it. I want to see this from every room."

I wasn't saying anything, but I had the oddest thing happen as I stood there listening to the two men and staring out over that expanse. I would turn around three hundred sixty degrees every now and then, just to look back at the plateau, the grama and the peaks with their piñon pines rising from the floor of the landscape. Betsy had her epiphany, and I seemed to be having my own in that very instant.

Bill laid out Betsy's requirements along with his own. "She wants three bedrooms, each with its own bath. We don't need any tubs—just showers. She wants one big living area with the kitchen open into it either on the side or end—doesn't matter. She wants a big laundry room with a pantry room big enough for a big chest freezer. We both want a large, covered porch going around the house—both to get out of the sun and to sit and stare at whichever view suits us at the time.

"Oh, and she wants a small chapel. It only needs to be big enough to seat twenty at the most and it can be, to use her words, 'simple as a Quaker meeting house.'

"I want a separate building for my office. The only luxury to that is for it to have a toilet and sink. I'm not gettin' any younger, and while I'd rather just pee outdoors, on cold or rainy days inside plumbing sounds pretty good."

We chuckled and Ernesto said, "Rosalinda won't let me pee outside in town. I don't know what her hang-up is. I told her she can pee in the yard—it wouldn't bother me."

We all chuckled again. I kept my peeing preferences to myself.

Bill asked, "What else you need to know?"

Ernesto said, "That'll get us started."

I wondered who "us" was. Was he already including me in the equation? I kinda hoped he was.

As he wrapped things up Bill said, "Now remember, you don't know nothin' about Betsy and her church situation. They'll figure it out when she's good and ready. I think Mr. Benson's book and this house might be what rebuilds this family. I'd like to bring Billy home, redeem that son of mine that sows his wild oats every chance he gets and welcome my daughter back into our home. I've never had a problem with the girls, but it would be an understatement to say that Betsy has. Mr. Benson seems to have cracked her heart open in that regard. I may have to write him a thank you letter when this is all done and the family is back in one piece. I just can't help but feel like this is the next step towards that—get out here on the ranch."

Radio *still* off, as we drove back to town, Ernesto said, "I had no idea that man ever had that much to say. If I ever heard more than two dozen words from him at one time, I can't recall when it would have been. It takes something to outtalk me."

"I was gonna say that," I said. "I mean the part about it taking something to outtalk you. You didn't even get a chance to work in a damn or a *caca* or an MF."

He looked over at me and said, "Maybe I'll clean up my act. If Ms. Schlatter can turn over a new leaf, maybe I should too."

"You want me to tell Rosalinda of your newfound vigor for a clean tongue?" I asked.

"Hell no!" he said laughing.

Then I asked him, "Have you designed houses before?"

"I've built them my whole life and would just as soon work from a sketch than fancy plans. It might take some back and forth, but I think we can come up with what we need for him."

I then revealed my epiphany of sorts. "While we were standing there, I had in my mind the house growing as he described the basics of what he wanted. If you don't mind, I'd like to see if I can take what I saw upstairs here in this claptrap brain of mine and get it onto paper. I don't have a computer to do anything professional like that."

"I just said I don't need fancy," he replied. "Go for it. I've got some drafting paper. We can stop by the house and get it before I drop you home."

Then he ended with, "Keep your day job until we know this is gonna take off."

"I planned to," I said.

And with that—the radio was back on, arm out the window and the "happy Mexican," as he often called himself, was singing his heart out.

Chapter Fourteen

I wasted no time. As soon as Ernesto dropped me off with drafting paper and scale rule in hand, I sat down at the kitchen table and started drawing a house. The evening turned into night and before I knew it the sun was coming up. I had put the house down on paper almost as if I was taking direction from some hand guiding mine. I'd never drawn a thing in my life and never considered drafting, architecture or engineering as any kind of career option.

Not only did I have floor plans, but I had some rough sketch of what each of the elevations would look like. As I was working on them, it occurred to me none of us had written anything down. Bill rattled off things from his memory and seemed to trust ours enough to get started on their ideas. It was all so fresh for me I was certain I'd captured everything he'd said. Well, my certainty was offset by the notion that I hoped I had at any rate. We'd know if Ernesto felt like we had something we could take to Bill.

On separate sheets I had Bill's office, complete with WC, and Betsy's chapel. Technically, I took one liberty with Bill's specifications. Two of the bedrooms were more of a separate wing of the house connected with a small library/sitting room/kitchenette, where I felt that if Billy came home, he'd have his own space.

I knew my landlords would be up and around getting ready for church by then so I knocked on their door.

The first thing Lupe said was, "We saw Ernesto haul you off yesterday and didn't see you come home. What no good thing was he trying to drag you into?"

I said, "I'll let him tell you that. It's safe to say it was 'all good' and not the 'no good' one might have had reason to suspect."

She said, "That's a relief."

I stated my purpose. "In fact, I wanted to see if I could borrow your phone to call him."

"Come on in," she said.

Rosalinda answered. "Is he up?" I asked.

"Up enough," she said. "Hang on....Ernesto! Phone!"

She didn't tell him who it was. By caller ID he thought it was Chuy. "Hey, *pendejo!*"

"Excuse me?" I said. I might have returned the salutation, but Lupe was well within range of hearing my end of the conversation if not his.

"Oh, I thought it was my brother."

"That's what you get for thinkin," I said. "Hey, I've got something sketched if you want to take a look to see if I'm heading anywhere good."

"I was skipping Mass today anyway. I'll come by as soon as I know Chuy and Lupe are gone."

"Sounds good," I said and hung up.

I sat down in my lawn chair to wait for Ernesto. He definitely knows their schedule. They hadn't been gone two minutes when he pulled in. I was surprised Rosalinda was with him—skipping Mass as well. He gave an upward nod of his head and said, "Bring what you got. We're gonna go up to the lodge for breakfast per the señora's orders."

I got up, rolled everything I had already laid out for him to see, grabbed a rubber band to keep it all tidy and got in the backseat of their crew-cap pickup. I don't think Ernesto had noticed the roll was several sheets.

When we got to the restaurant, I set the roll on the chair beside me. We ordered and finished our breakfast after he had revealed in the course of the conversation what was clear he'd told Rosalinda about the previous day and to some degree what he had not.

All she said about the revelations was, "I haven't had to take a vow of silence before."

Ernesto looked around to see if we could look at what I had then and there, or if we needed to go somewhere else. He said, "There's nobody here who's gonna know what we're doing. As soon as we can get the table cleared, let's see what you got."

The waitress came and cleared off the table and gave it a quick wipe-down at Rosalinda's request.

I unrolled the plans, already stacked in the order I wanted him to see them.

"Holy *caca, hombre*! Did you work on these all night?"

"That would be pretty accurate," I said.

He went from the floor plan to the next page with two of the elevations, then to the next two and finally to the chapel and office page before going back to the main floor plan.

He asked for confirmation, "And you've never drawn a house or built anything before?"

"No," I said simply enough.

He said it again, "You've never drawn a house or built anything before?"

I smiled and said, "Honestly, no I haven't."

"What do you think, *mujer*?" he asked his wife.

She said, "I think he's gonna spare you some embarrassment for what you might have shown Bill and Betsy."

"Damn straight!" he replied as he began to study each page in more detail. Seeing the separation of the wings he said, "It looks like you made that so Billy could move right in."

"I'm glad it looks that way to you," I said. "That was the idea I had, putting it off on its own wing but still keeping the porches Bill wanted."

Rosalinda studied the chapel plan a bit and said, "I've never seen a chapel designed like that. It is quite unique. I really like it. You even show the furniture layout."

Ernesto said, "Let's get goin.' I'm gonna try to get a hold of Bill when I can get a cell signal since I can't up here. On the Sundays he goes to church, he goes to the Methodist church he grew up in. They should be out soon. I'll see when we might get together next."

I rolled the plans back up and reached for my wallet to pay for my breakfast.

Rosalinda saw the wallet and said, "Put that away. There's no way you're paying for your breakfast this morning."

As soon as we got on the edge of town, Ernesto pulled off the side of the road to try Bill's cell number. Bill obviously knew Ernesto's number and Ernesto had turned up the volume hoping we all could hear both sides of the conversation.

"Howdy," Bill said. "Calling to tell me it's a no go on the tractor deal?"

Ernesto said, "*Jaime* has some ideas on plans. Rosalinda and I have just taken a look at them. I think you should take a look and see if we're on the right track. If that sounds okay, let me know when you might want to meet."

Bill said, "We're here if you want to come over now. No time like the present."

Ernesto felt the need to clarify "now." He said, "We're all three in the truck just coming from breakfast. Now could mean in two minutes we'd be there."

"That sounds good. Come on. We'll put some fresh coffee on." And with that Bill hung up. No goodbye or see you in a bit.

Ernesto said, "I guess now is now, " and headed over to the Schlatter home.

Chapter Fifteen

In the minute-thirty-seconds it took us to get from where we were to the Schlatters, I said I'd still never met Betsy and wasn't at all sure I'd seen her around—though I probably had.

Rosalinda said, "She's been in the Slo Poke Cafe when we've been there so you probably have, and we just didn't think to point her out."

She was right. Betsy answered the door, and I immediately recognized her from the restaurant. It was clear that whatever judgmental attitudes she had held over the years, basic gentility and hospitality were traits ingrained in her from childhood. She very politely welcomed us and led us into the den. Bill emerged from the backyard having stepped out to smoke one of his King Edwards.

Bill started, "I've assured Betsy that you've all taken an oath to keep our business between ourselves for a bit until she has a chance to sort things out with her church friends."

Ernesto said, "We're not telling anyone. You know Rosalinda's not going to say anything. *Jaime* here will do the same. I'm the only big mouth, and I promise as well."

Betsy simply said, "I appreciate it."

Ernesto proceeded by saying, "*Jaime* here, who says he's never drawn a house or built anything, wanted to take a stab at laying out some ideas. No point in doing much more if it's not at all what you have in mind."

And with that introduction he rolled the plans out before the "prospective clients."

Neither one said a word. They spent a good five minutes looking at the main floor plan, then studied each of the elevations and finally turned to the last page with the office and chapel. At that point, Betsy got up rather abruptly and went quickly into another part of the house.

Bill stood up and said, "Excuse me just a moment."

He was gone two—maybe three minutes. We sat there rather uncomfortably hoping we hadn't unintentionally offended her in some way. We certainly couldn't talk about it, but afterward the three of us confirmed the same thing was running through our minds.

Bill came back and sat down with us, flipping from the last page back to the first. He sighed and said, "You did her in. She couldn't hold back the tears. She'll be back out in a minute or two.

"Let me get that coffee I promised." And he was off to the kitchen.

He arrived with the coffee at the same time Betsy reappeared refreshed and composed. She smiled brightly at us and said, "We'd like to hang onto these and study them carefully. We'll make notes of things as we think of them. Let me say, I don't know how you stood on a ridge for maybe an hour yesterday and then went home and did all this, but it's like you knew what we wanted when we didn't know ourselves."

Bill said, "Let's get to it. Ernesto, when could you start work. How backed up are you?"

Ernesto said, "I've got a job to finish this week and the next big job in line has been dragging their feet. I have no problem telling them they missed the boat for a while."

Bill asked, "Other than a plumber, electrician and the steel for the roof, what other help are you going to need to get it all built?"

Ernesto answered, "I'll need some extra hands when we're seriously making adobes and for the staining, roof structure and Saltillos, but nothing that would run more than $25-30 an hour for the extra labor on top of my $75 an hour rate for me and my crew."

Bill said, "That's sound about right. I'll set up accounts here in town and in Alpine for materials including the concrete. Jaime, you gonna work on this project too?"

"Yes, sir, that's what Ernesto and I have discussed."

"Good," Bill said. "Both of you will be set up then to order things as needs be. And I'll give Jerry the go-ahead this week to get the tractors delivered."

Betsy slipped into the kitchen and was back in a minute to fill our coffee cups. While pouring, she looked at Rosalinda mostly, but Ernesto was meant to be included as well it seemed. She said, "I'm sorry I've been such a bitch all these years. Bill, roll up those plans for now."

She was gone another couple minutes and returned with a platter filled with chips and salsa, fresh veggies, and warm tamales. Bill, seeing the tamales said, "I'd better have a beer. Who'll join me?"

Everyone but Betsy as it turned out, though she did take a sip of Bill's, which surprised him more than us. She just shook her head with that sour-face that comes when one hasn't developed a taste for beer.

Back in the truck, Ernesto said, "You know how I said you'd better keep that day job? You'd better give your notice. Looks like we're gonna get busy pretty quick."

"Chuy will certainly be surprised," I said.

Ernesto replied, "Yeah, we gotta tell him enough to get you taken care of without betraying the Schlatter's confidence. That might be a little tricky, but since my helper just left, I have a good excuse. We'll talk to them when we drop you off."

Then he said, "I didn't want to be a pig, but the little bit of tamales I ate just made me hungrier."

He'd no sooner said that when his cell phone rang. We could only hear his half of the conversation. "Yes, sir," followed by a long silence. "I don't know either. We hadn't talked about it." Another silence. "That sounds fair. I'm sure he'd appreciate it." More silence. "No, you won't be able to get him on the phone. He doesn't have one, but he's here with me now. I'll ask him.

"Bill feels bad that they didn't properly thank you for your work or offer anything for your time. They were too surprised to think straight. He wants to know if $500 is fair for the work you've done so far."

I reached up to the front seat so that Ernesto could hand me his phone. "Hi, Mr. Schlatter. It's Jaime. That's very generous, but you don't owe me anything. Study the plans and you might decide you want something different. I'm glad to help in whatever way I can. Besides it looks like I'll be working with Ernesto on the buildings—that's compensation enough for me."

Bill said, "You need to call me Bill and not Mr. Schlatter. And I think we ought to pay you something now, but at least I wanted to say thank you, so thank you."

"You are most welcome," I said. "Did you want to talk to Ernesto again?"

"No," Bill said. "That was all for the moment. Y'all have a good Sunday. Betsy and I are fixin' to sit down to lunch with some more of these tamales."

"They sure were good. We'll see you soon, and take care." With that I handed the phone back to Ernesto, who put the phone to his ear just to be sure Bill had hung up.

Since we had already arrived at the casita, Chuy and Lupe were standing there looking at us, wondering why we were sitting in the truck, motor running, windows up and passing the phone around. Ernesto lowered his window and asked, "You two want to go to the Slo Poke Cafe for lunch?"

Chuy looked at his watch and said, "It's probably packed by now. We've got plenty of brisket. Why don't you all come in for lunch."

Ernesto turned his head a bit towards Rosalinda and me, winked and said, "Got the free lunch I was really after." He turned off the engine, and we headed into the house.

Chapter Sixteen

We were no sooner in the house when Chuy said, "Y'all have been up to something this weekend. I don't know what it is, but I know you've been scheming about something."

Ernesto said, "I told you Charlie quit on me and moved to Midland. I've talked *Jaime* into coming to work for me."

Lupe asked, "Do you have enough to keep him busy? I thought that big job you thought was coming hasn't made any start to get you out there."

He replied, "I got some fill-in work to tide us over. Looks like we got some more work lined up yesterday."

"Who for?" Chuy asked.

"Won't say until it's a done deal," Ernesto said.

Chuy asked me, "So are you turning in your notice tomorrow?"

"Looks like it," I said. "I want to give two weeks if you think that's all right."

Chuy said, "You know as well as I that two weeks is a courtesy few extend out there. Most just quit coming to work. If you're not riding with me, who's gonna buy my gas to get back and forth to work?"

I said, "I just hope you don't evict me or go up too much on the rent. I'm not sure how much your brother's gonna pay me. We forgot to get around to talkin' money."

Lupe said, "No wonder he can afford you. He hasn't promised you anything."

Rosalinda said, "We'll do right by him, I'll promise him that."

Then Chuy said, "You're going to be missed out at the tomato farm, but you don't have to worry about an eviction notice."

"I appreciate that very much. What a lifesaver you two were when I arrived here with my peanut butter and not enough money to pay the rent."

We'd told Lupe and Chuy just enough for me to do what needed to be done on Monday when I went into work without revealing the fuller extent of what would unfold over the next few weeks. I was rather eager to get back to my room—having been up all night—and so, as soon as we finished eating, I excused myself. I

69

laid down to take a nap and as happens, tired though the body was, the mind wouldn't quite shut down long enough to allow the sleep I wanted to come to me.

My mind returned to that beautiful ranch with its herd of cattle that looked like an imagined, idealized landscape yet was very real. I was surprised how many cattle were out on the range—I couldn't count them as we drove past—not only the cattle but a large herd of antelope coexisting with their fellow ruminants turning cellulose into protein-dense muscle. Something the big-brain mammals who claim dominion over them cannot do.

I had mostly ignored California agriculture like most city-folk—truth be told. Californians may get wound up from time to time about the water use that heavily irrigated "farms" require, but at the same time, they want non-disrupted inventories of almond milk, strawberries and salads in their 24/7/365 grocery stores.

Working at the tomato farm, I had really become more analytical in my reflections back to those huge monoculture, irrigated strawberry fields I would pass, where they grew berries on the backs of cheap labor—strawberries bigger than golfballs with the near taste and texture of artificially flavored cardboard.

That was always my impression of hothouse-tomatoes as well—though the Dutch seem to have a much better formula for keeping a reasonable-sized fruit and flavorful tomato than most of the competition. Still, I looked at the tomato farm that sustained me and questioned its context to place. We certainly had plenty of sunshine so it wasn't altogether a mystery why they picked the West Texas desert for their operations. But miles and miles of transport were required to get the efficient bounty of the place to the produce shelves where the red fruits would turn the profits needed for their owners.

It required drawing heavily from what are certainly limited aquifers. However, when a good summer thunderstorm brewed, it seemed a most precarious place to be. In fact, just a few weeks earlier on July 5th, we'd had a hail storm that didn't do major damage but did enough. It certainly sent workers out in the greenhouse running for cover in our part of the operation, and it left a hell of a mess to deal with and panels of glass to replace. I wondered then, what happens when a real hail storm hits this place? I had to presume that was a "when not if" question. It would be a disaster. The workers would be picking up glass shards instead of fruit for weeks if not months. Or as seemed more likely to me, the Dutch would abandon it out of the need to file bankruptcy or simply to cut their losses and move on. Left behind would be what we see too often of past "industrial production" facilities, which is a derelict, abandoned relic—a blight on the landscape for as far into the future as one can imagine as no one can make an economic justification for cleaning up the mess.

The one positive thought I had in that regard was that at least recycling has come a long way in recent years, and there was enough metal to perhaps make some second life possible for the shell of the place. All that entered my mind just from those few broken panels on July 5th and was now replaying in my tired body and woken mind. I finally resigned myself to the fact I was too wound up to sleep. I went back outside and sat in my lawn chair— that is, until another summer thunderstorm finally drove me back inside when the show of rumbling thunder and lightning flashes turned into a huge downpour. I stood in my doorway watching it wash all the dust off everything in sight—leaving Fort Davis, for a brief time, looking as though it had just gone through the car wash.

When the sun finally went to bed, so did I. I was asleep before my head hit the pillow—and I don't even remember a single dream that night. I awoke refreshed and both eager and apprehensive— after these last few years of some constancy in my life—as to my fate unfolding yet again before me.

Chapter Seventeen

The manager of the Fort Davis tomato farm was certainly used to dealing with turnover. Not only did he take my resignation in stride, he layered on top of it a healthy dose of generosity. Since in all the time I'd worked there I'd only taken two days off, he suggested I could take both my weeks notice as vacation or he'd pay me out in cash—my choice. I suggested a week of each, so I'd work one week, and then I'd be free to start working with Ernesto the second week.

I knew that my routine of helping at the pantry the two Saturdays a month might well have to change as it was likely there would be at least some Saturdays when we'd be working. In fact, Bill wanted us to come to meet him at the ranch this Saturday, which was a distribution day at the pantry. Ernesto told him we'd be there around ten, and Bill said he'd meet us at the cattle guard.

I had noticed on our trip out there the week earlier that as we came to a "Y" in the ranch road, there were fence rows perpendicular going off in both directions just before the "Y" as well as a cattle guard in both directions where the road split with yet another fence row continuing straight down between the two. I suspected, and Ernesto confirmed, that to the left was Sallie's part of the ranch. Neither maintained any signage whatsoever. And there was no name or number on the mailbox though each had one. Those were simply drop-off points so that Bill could drop off Sallie's mail when he'd come out to the ranch, or if Sallie had something to get to Bill, she'd put it in his mailbox. They'd use the flag to signal something was in the box for the other.

It would be almost impossible for the United States Postal Service to provide local mailbox service out in this part of the world, but it doesn't seem to me they make much effort compared to what passes for acceptable service in the rest of the country. You either get your mail in town, or a few "communities" drive to a row of mailboxes along the road clumped in groups on what they called their highway carrier route. The closest one could be miles from your home. Either way, you are assigned a box number—either a PO box if in town or an HC box—a highway carrier box in the country. They would give you a no-charge PO box in town but it is the size of half a small shoe box. When you only get your mail once a week or less, it is pretty useless. To get a bigger box means paying for it. Even people living in town often spring for one of the bigger boxes ranging from double the size of the small box to file-drawer size.

It seemed to me some uninformed bureaucrat is leading the design and construction of these cookie-cutter post offices. If they understood life in these remote parts of the country, everyone would have large, free mailboxes, which still saves them the legions of mail carriers needed in their cities. The one-time expense of a little infrastructure just seemed to me the right thing to do knowing it isn't likely to ever come about. The government is pretty good at cookie-cutter and not too good at looking at the context of place—one more example of how context to place keeps swirling in my mind since moving here.

Bill was waiting for us at the cattle guard and we followed him past the ramshackle and pens, where we saw his new tractor. About a quarter mile past there, he turned off onto another one of the roads in the ranch where we drove two or three miles before we spotted the big new John Deere with its front end loader and backhoe.

As soon as Ernesto saw it he said, "*Ah, una chica guapa!*"

I agreed, "She is a pretty thing."

We joined Bill who had walked over to a small pit cut into the land. He said, "This is where they dug the clay for the adobe they used on the ranch back in the day. I thought you should check it out to see if you think it will work for the adobes we need."

He handed a set of keys to Ernesto adding, "I'm not suggesting you have to do anything about it this minute—I just wanted the tractor back here so you have it to dig around some and decide if we're in luck or need to explore elsewhere."

Then he headed back towards his truck as we followed. He reached in to get the plans I'd drawn and laid them out on the hood of his pickup. It was the perfect viewing platform for the tall, lanky rancher but a little bit high for Ernesto and me.

Instead of marking them all up, he had a legal pad he laid up alongside the plans. He said, "It would be an understatement to say we have spent some time with these this week. Betsy forgot to make dinner two different nights she was so engrossed in building this house. I had to eat canned tuna, and I don't even like tuna.

"You'll see our notes are really just details of finish-out—a lot of details as you will see." Looking at me he said, "It appeared from your elevations that you were trying to avoid any exposed wood outside. Did we read that correctly?"

I said, "Yes, I thought that for two reasons. One was the UV we get here at this altitude and the dry air eats up wood pretty quickly, but I thought of equal, maybe even more importance, was to make the buildings as fireproof as possible in case of a wildfire."

He responded, "That's great. Betsy asked about some wood here and there, and I said exactly that—they'd just be something that could catch fire if we ever had a big fire come across the ranch."

He rolled up the plans and handed them to me along with the legal pad. "You two study 'em, and let us know what questions or concerns you have. As far as we're concerned, we've got enough to get started whenever you're ready to break ground. Let us know, and Betsy and I will come out to help stake things out to be sure it sits right where we want."

Just as Bill was getting in the truck he stopped, "Oh, we forgot to talk about a septic system. You probably noticed we do have a well and electricity to the ridge but we don't have any septic back there." Looking at Ernesto he asked, "I assume your brother Rogelio will do that work?"

Ernesto said, "Having the tractor out here, I'll do all the dirt work, but we'll need him to handle the county permit and inspection process. I'll talk to him as soon as you say we're good to let folks know we're building out here."

"Damn! I forgot to even mention that," Bill exclaimed. "It's official. By this afternoon the whole town will know, and Betsy will be cast out into the outer darkness by her church. She and our daughter and her partner were all going to the food pantry this morning to help out. Betsy said, 'I can't think of a stronger message to send that times are a-changin' than for me to show up there with my gay daughter and her lover.'"

With that, he was as amused at his retelling of her morning plans as we were surprised to hear them. Then he said, "By the way, she wanted us to meet her at the Slo Poke Cafe when we get back into town. She figured she'd get there before us but would grab a big enough table for us and Rosalinda, assuming she'll join us too since we know that's your regular food pantry day lunch spot."

We were all off to the Slo Poke Cafe. I told Ernesto on the way, "I can't wait to hear Rosalinda's account of Betsy and the girls all showing up together to volunteer. I'll bet Emma nearly had a stroke after being told by Betsy so many times what an embarrassment the pantry was to the community all these years."

Ernesto said, "I'd have paid admission to see it!"

I asked Ernesto, "What's their daughter's name and do you know her partner's?"

He said, "The daughter is Jean and the partner is Mary-Alice. They have a bookkeeping business they run together. I don't think they've had many Fort Davis clients, thanks to Betsy, but they have all the work they can handle from Marfa and Alpine from what I gather from Rosalinda.

"She says they are well-matched—that they look like bookends except that Jean, like her dad, is tall and lanky and about as flat-chested as a woman *can* be, and Mary-Alice is also tall but, as she puts it, 'with more than adequate endowment up there.' As best we can tell they plug along with no hostility from the community. They work together, pray together and stay together. That's better than most marriages ever do."

I said, "It's frightening to have such subversive women lurking about. Episcopalians and accountants—what's the world coming to?"

Chapter Eighteen

Betsy and Rosalinda were indeed there waiting for us at the Slo Poke Cafe. In addition to the two of them were Jean, Mary-Alice and Emma. I didn't need any introduction to Jean to realize which one was the Schlatter. She was tall, lanky and looked like a female version of Bill. Both too were in starched, white shirts and stiff bluejeans. Being the only unknown of the group, I was properly introduced by Bill to the girls.

I sat next to Emma who leaned over to me and whispered, "Will wonders never cease?"

I certainly knew the cat was out of the bag regarding the new house. Betsy said loud enough for anyone near to hear and which Sara for sure heard, "Jean and Mary-Alice want to come out to the ranch when we stake off where the new house is going to go."

In fact, Sara stopped with her arms loaded with hot plates to ask Betsy, "Are you going to move out to the ranch?"

Betsy said, "Jaime here has designed a beautiful house, office and even a chapel, and Ernesto and he are going to get busy building it. I doubt it will be ready as a Christmas present, but maybe we'll be in by Easter."

Ernesto said, "I can guarantee you won't be in by Christmas, and whether you're in by Easter will depend on the weather as much or more as it will the crew building it." Then he added with a smile, "I guess I should look at the calendar to see if Easter is early or late this year."

After Sara set down the hot plates she'd been holding, she came back over to speak to me. "I didn't know you designed houses."

I said, "I didn't know I did either."

Betsy said, "He had a sudden inspiration, and as I haven't done enough in my life, he decided to act while the spirit was moving."

I thought Betsy might be taken aback if she understood how unreligious my background really was and how much I still struggled with matters of faith. But I had no problem agreeing with her that some spirit had moved, and I moved with it.

It was rather surreal to sit there with this group who only a week or two earlier had coexisted along side each other their entire lives with virtually no polite contact between them for years. In that regard, Rosalinda was perhaps the one ambassador of goodwill who had been able to interact with all of them at least at some level of courtesy—though even to that point, I recalled Betsy's apology to Rosalinda for being a bitch. Now, we sat as a convivial, lighthearted bunch of very different people, and my misfit self began to feel just that tad bit more part of the larger community beyond the Cardonas—though still, all my integration came down to their inclusion of me in their lives.

As though the day hadn't been extraordinary enough already, in walks Sallie—jeans, cowgirl boots and spurs. She hung her wide-brimmed hat on the hat rack by the door and headed our way. She pulled up another chair to squeeze in by her sister, which I think surprised Betsy as she usually only dealt with Bill.

She saw Sara and said, "Hi, Sara. How ya doin'? I'd like an ice tea and the beef taco plate. I appreciate it." Courteous as she was, she didn't really wait to hear Sara's answer to her question, and I gathered Sara was used to Sallie rattling off her order in a similar manner.

To her sister she said, "What's this I hear about you moving to the ranch? I was just in the post office and overheard a couple women from that church of yours who said you'd gone over to the devil. I couldn't help myself and asked what you'd done now. They said you'd accepted your homosexual daughter and were moving to the ranch.

"I thought, I hope you're not coming to live with me, since I couldn't see you livin' in the bunkhouse and there's nothing else to live in out there except with me. Family is family, but I'm not sure we're ready to live together just yet. I saw your car in the parking lot along with Bill's truck so here I am to get caught up on the family drama."

Then she shot back up before Betsy could say a word and reached over to shake Jean and Mary-Alice's hands clearly showing that she'd not estranged herself from them even if they saw each other rarely. Then taking in everyone at the table, she realized she didn't know me or Emma, and came to introduce herself before taking her seat by her sister to get the answer to the family news and how the devil had seized her. You could tell from her handshake that those hands had worked hard all their life. I could see her out roping calves and wiping sweat from her forehead where the hat band set squarely on her head. I liked her immediately!

Betsy said, "Believe it or not, I was going to call you this afternoon and have a long talk. Yes, my church thinks I'm lost, but in getting lost, I'm finding my own children. I hope to have all of them back in our lives. I see what a fool I've been. Me living out on the ranch—you never imagined that, did you? No, I'm not moving in with you. Ernesto and Jaime are going to build us a house out on that ridge that has always been Bill's dream spot. We already have it pretty well laid out and hope to get going on it any day now. It all moved pretty fast—much faster than we could have imagined."

It seems folk who deal with livestock can talk about death easier than most. Sallie said, "It could be we'll get your final rest out on that ridge where Momma and Daddy are buried. Daddy always wanted that though he assumed you'd be buried here in town."

Betsy said, "I'm just building a house! I didn't think I was ready to go into a box yet. But if it makes you feel any better, I have considered selling our plots here in town."

Bill was surprised by that. "Really? Suits me fine!"

Jean looked at Mary-Alice with a look that made me think she was saying silently to her partner—what next? One person's simple change of heart was changing so much for so many so quickly.

Lunch all done, back in the parking lot Betsy got the plans from me to show Sallie. While they looked them over, Ernesto told Bill he wanted to them take over to the university and get copies made so they could be marked up for measurements, plumbing, electric and notes for the different details on the finish-out. Then he'd also get out to the ranch to get into that adobe pit and see how things stood. Lastly, he wanted Bill to set a date for meeting there to set the lay lines.

We waited while Bill went over to the two sisters and soon was back with the plans. He said, "Weather permitting let's meet out there a week from today at 10:00 to stake things out. Call if you have to change the time, and I'll do the same."

"*Bueno*," Ernesto said.

Ernesto got the copies made on Monday and stopped in after he knew I'd be back from the tomato farm.

He gave his new employee his first instructions. "You've got the scale rule and write better than I do. Take one set and mark it up just with the dimensions. That one we need by Saturday so we're sure to get everything right. Then take two sets and mark them up with all their notes off on the side—room by room. One of those will be for them and one for us. I'm going to keep two copies —one for the plumber and one for the electrician. We don't really need to do anything on that just yet. Mostly we'll mark things as we go. They'd rather work that way anyway. Like me, fancy plans just slow 'em down."

I had no problem getting all my homework done well before the Saturday deadline.

Chapter Nineteen

We didn't have to worry about the weather on that first Saturday in September. It was a calm, cloudless day with that big blue West Texas sky that takes your breath away. By the time we arrived at the ridge, Betsy and Bill were already there, which didn't surprise us. Jean and Mary-Alice were also there, as was Sallie. There was one other young man as well. I asked Ernesto, "Is that Billy?"

Ernesto said, "No, that's the other son, the middle child—Brett. They don't have to worry about Jean and Billy givin' 'em grandkids —he's given them several they know about and no tellin' how many they don't."

I said, "I'd heard from Chuy and Lupe he was on the wild side. I never asked where he lives."

Ernesto said, "El Paso last I knew. He was in Alpine before he ran out of women."

I then asked, "Are you surprised he's here?"

"Hell, *mi amigo*, nothing right now with this family would surprise me," he said laughingly.

Bill had seen to it that any vehicles were well out of our way, and Ernesto backed in where the stakes and batter boards he wanted to get in today would be handy to grab. Then he said, "We only need them to agree on the front line and angle of each building. After that they can stay or go as they see fit. You and I are going to keep after it until we get as much laid out today as possible. I'll have to scrape the grass and do some fill, but I want all the corners laid out to be sure I know what I need where and so I disturb as little grass as possible. And remind me to talk to Bill about the adobe pit."

"Is it going to work?" I asked.

"*Si señor.* As best I can tell at this point."

He didn't need a reminder. It was the first thing on Bill's mind. Bill said, "I was over at the pit before coming up here and see you did some digging and made several piles. I take that as a good sign. Am I right?"

Ernesto said, "Yes, I think we're in good shape and plan to get going on those quickly while we've got good weather. The rains should be mostly gone any day now."

Bill agreed, "Yes, I miss the rains when they leave, but don't see much coming our way for a while. You'll probably have it all done by Christmas just because the weather's so good. Hell, I might even buy you a new pickup to go with that tractor if you pull it off."

Ernesto said, "I'll be driving this old truck for a few more years then."

Bill said, "I know it can't happen by Christmas. I'm just givin' ya a hard time since that's what Betsy said at the Slo Poke."

Ernesto grabbed his long tape measure and roll of string. He said we'd need the transit but not yet. He motioned for me to grab some stakes and the mallet. Bill asked what he could carry and Ernesto asked him to get the drawing marked up with the dimensions from the cab.

Betsy seemed to be planted in one place and not staring out over the ridge like the rest of the family. Bill headed towards her and we followed. Without turning to us she said, "Right here is where I picture the chapel and I'd like it turned at forty-five degrees from the other buildings so that those stair-stepped, side windows Jaime drew face out to the mountains here to the east. Look how beautiful this is. When I sit in the chapel early in the morning, I can watch the sun come up over the mountains and even at sunset, I'll see that pink in the eastern sky that so often comes with dusk here."

Ernesto glanced at the dimensional plans that Bill was holding and moved to a spot and said to Betsy, "That would put the door right about here. Does that look right to you?"

She answered, "Perfect."

Ernesto said, "*Jaime*, drive a stake right here."

The natural world must have approved. Just as we were about to move from the spot Bill said, "Look just over there. They seem to be signing off on the plan."

He was looking toward a small herd of mule deer and just past them a dozen antelope that had assembled off to the southeast and were all looking at us gathered in the "chapel".

Betsy said, "If the budget allows it, I'd like to have a rock wall all the way around the chapel—not so tall it blocks the view. I'd like to have a small rose garden inside the walls." She looked at me thinking I might not know this. "Roses do surprisingly well here in the desert mountains."

I said, "I've noticed that from several I've seen in town. I've even planted a couple at my apartment."

Ernesto was wise enough not to make a promise he might regret so he said nothing to ensure the wall would be in the package. Bill didn't encourage it or discourage it. Both the "project manager," Bill, and the "builder," Ernesto, found it best to move onto the house site as they headed to where the others were still assembled.

I was just a few steps behind them as I paused long enough to take in for a moment longer the eastern view Betsy had framed in her mind from the chapel window. "An inspired choice," I said out loud to myself.

It didn't take us but five minutes to run a string line across where the front of the porch would run and out to the far corners on each end. We then spotted where Bill wanted his office.

Once we had the string lines for the house and office in place, Ernesto said to the group, "*Jaime* and I need to get to work on laying everything out. It's a two-man job, so if you stay or go it's up to you."

With that he was off to get his transit set up and told me where to put piles of stakes and batter boards. With the transit set up he also got more string and a couple cans of orange spray paint. He jokingly said to Bill, "I need you to put your hand on the ground at the two front corners we marked so I can spray over them as proof you approved the spot the house goes. It will be like a handprint in the cement. Might not be permanent like cement, but I'll take a picture of it for proof."

Bill said, "How about if I just stand here smiling and you take a picture?"

Ernesto said, "I guess that would work, too."

No picture was taken by Ernesto, but for prosperity Jean took one of her mom and dad on each of the front corners—both grinning widely in each shot. Brett was standing next to Jean and whispered, "I'm not sure I've ever seen them as bright-eyed as they are right now."

Jean whispered back, "I know. I keep wanting to ask, 'What have you done with my mother?'"

Betsy saw them whispering and laughing amongst themselves and asked, "Anything you want to share with the group?"

Jean was quick on her feet and said, "Just how happy we are to be a family again."

Bill said to Betsy so we all could hear, "Yeah—I'm sure that's what they were chucklin' about. More likely getting amused at our expense."

Ernesto and I got busy and the family stayed around watching and visiting for another hour or so before they all headed off the ranch and Sallie back to her own. She'd come over on horseback and rode off in a gentle trot as I imagined how that was so characteristic of many of her days. I couldn't see her riding a "gator" UTV around checking out things on the ranch. I thought how disappointed I'd be if such was actually the case.

In fairly short order, we had both the office and chapel laid out. It was almost dark before we had the more complex corners of the main house all done. Ernesto said, "The 'architect' could have made this a little easier to lay out. He sure likes corners and angles —on both the chapel and house."

I replied, "Isn't it the truth? Those guys never build anything, so if it looks pretty on the page, that's all they care about."

Chapter Twenty

As I thought about adobe making, the only real picture I had in my mind was wives stomping in bare feet in the mud and straw, mixing it together for their husbands to come get the mud, bucket by bucket, and put it in molds to dry in the sun. Naturally with that image in mind, I saw me as the mud stomper and Ernesto the mud former working on adobes for months on end. I thought to have enough to build a house would take until Easter before we laid them into the first wall. Sometimes the ignorance of the uninitiated is best left to silence. I decided rather than ask Ernesto how we would be going about such a task, it was best just to wait and see.

Unbeknownst to me, he had a separate piece of property up behind town where he kept the industrial side of his operation. I had just assumed we'd be making the adobes out on the ranch next to the pit though I did wonder how we were going to get the water needed. Bill's pit was for the raw material and that was it. In town, Ernesto's setup included stacks and stacks of forms, a huge flat drying area, the mixer part of an old cement truck—which he had powered by its own motor to do all the mixing—a materials elevator to carry the material into the mixer, and a shed full of bags of cement plus some piles of sand and gravel.

He explained the process and formula on this, my first official day on my new job. "You probably figured out the other day that Rogelio is licensed to install septic systems. Our other brother, Mando, has his own dump truck. He is going to be hauling in the clay from Bill's pit to our yard here so we can get to making the adobes.

"If we keep the adobes to less than 30% clay, then we don't need any straw. I don't know why the Hebrews felt mistreated when Pharaoh said, 'Make bricks with no straw.' The more clay the more they'll crack. The rest of the mix is sand, gravel, and if you can get your hands on it, crushed granite. That would be a pretty traditional mix. Some people have started to make papercrete blocks, which they get from a cardboard mash. They are a lot lighter. I'd like to try that sometime, but you need lots of cardboard I'm not sure I could get my hands on in short order, and I don't want to experiment on the Schlatters. Some people even use asphalt in the blocks, but if you don't get the right grade of that, you're gonna think you live in a tar factory. I've never risked it.

"I use cement since I don't have granite dust, and it offers the advantage that you can plaster it or not. It doesn't matter. It hardens the adobe enough to not have to worry about it wearing down in the weather. Old mud adobe will go back to dirt if left exposed long enough.

"And since I like to leave the option of exposed adobes, I do throw in some fiberglass to protect against any cracks. *Entienda?*"

"*Si, entiendo.*" Not only did I understand, I was rather surprised by his very instructive method in laying it all out.

Then he continued, "As you can see, I've still got some sand and gravel on hand. I've got Mando out getting us a load of clay this morning. I had my own pit I could dig out of for several years, but the best of that is pretty well shot. I'm glad he had a good spot to dig from. Not everyone wants a big hole in their property even if they want an adobe house. Somehow they think somebody else should provide the hole for them not to have to look at it."

"Same with landfills, of course," I said. "Everyone has garbage —no one wants the landfill in their county."

"*Exactamente,*" he replied.

Three of the helpers Ernesto had lined up pulled in just then, and about ten minutes later Mando arrived with his first load of clay.

Mando said, "I'll get another load right away, then I've got to haul some gravel over by Alpine. Then I'll get some more hauled late this afternoon."

"*Bueno,*" was all Ernesto said.

He had an old Bobcat with thread-bare tires, which he used just in the yard to move material around. Roberto, one of the helpers, knew how to drive it and had clearly helped numerous times before. Without being asked he hopped in and got to bringing the number of buckets needed for Ernesto's recipe as it went up into the cement mixer. I knew the hard part was about to descend on the project. Ernesto was up top on the mixer looking in adding water, letting it mix, then adding more until he was satisfied with the look of it.

I had followed the lead of the other two helpers, Manuel and Sergio, as we laid all the forms out on the ground. Every form made four blocks. Then they each grabbed a wheelbarrow, as did I, as we lined up at the chute of the mixer. Roberto was off the Bobcat. His job was to follow the three of us to be sure the fill was good and smoothed out.

Ernesto came down quickly off the platform and hollered, "Okay, *chicas*, here she comes!"

I just copied exactly what Manuel and Sergio did before me, though when it came to putting the mud in the forms, their experience was paying a big dividend. They were doing two to three wheelbarrows to my one. I thought maybe Ernesto would say something about it—either a chastisement to get a move on or just to rib the novice adobe maker. He did neither, which I took as a sign he knew I was doing the best I could and didn't want to call me out even in jest in front of people I didn't know.

Four yards of mud is a lot of mud! And that's with the mixer just about half full. It took us close to an hour to get it all in the forms. An hour of nonstop heavy gettin' after it! I got a little closer to keeping up but never quite got to one-on-one with my two coworkers.

I could see this work wasn't going to be quite like the tomato farm. Ernesto called break time and tossed each of us a Bud from the refrigerator he kept in the cement shed. "*Solamente uno, chicas.*"

I was surprised how quickly we pulled the forms off the wet mud. They were rinsed off and laid out for the next batch.

Ernesto announced, "Okay *muchachas*! Let's get to making adobes!"

When the second batch was done and forms removed and cleaned we laid them out for the next day's pour. Ernesto said, "*Hombres*, 600 down—11,400 to go!"

After the extra help had left for the day, Ernesto explained the rest of the process. Curing takes a while, but his plan was to get as many stacked and drying as possible in the next three weeks, and while they cured, he, Roberto and I would be out digging the foundations and pouring the concrete. He gave them a light spray down before leaving and said he would do that again early on Tuesday, explaining, "Shit dries quick here—the air is so dry."

I went home whupped! I had worked hard at the tomato farm but I discovered on that Monday just how many muscles had lain dormant that were now being summoned to the task at hand. I thought it worth noting that I'd gotten through an entire day without Ernesto hollering, "*Pendejo*, what the hell you doing?"

I also did the simple math—12,000 adobes, 600 per day, done in three weeks—looks like we'll be working Saturdays and at *least* two Sundays. While I thought rain would give us a break, I hoped we'd get them to drying as well.

The next morning Ernesto said, "I see you came back for more fun. I thought you might decide tomato packing looked pretty good."

I said, "How does a boy beat getting paid to play in the mud."

He replied, "Everybody seems to think I'm payin' you. I thought you were payin' me for the education. That university in Alpine gets big bucks to pass out what they know, and they don't know half what I do."

Even with his obvious self-evident exaggeration, I had to think on some level that was more of a truth in more ways than he'd ever know.

Chapter Twenty-one

By Sunday afternoon, like good Hebrews, we'd made our quota of bricks without straw—4,000 down, 8,000 to go. I didn't even want a beer. I just wanted to go to the casita and sit in my chair with a big glass of ice water followed by a second and a third. Chuy and Lupe came out to join me.

"Did my brother treat you all right? We haven't filled your job yet at the tomato farm. You can always come back."

I said, "Other than the fact he thinks I should pay him for all the education he's providing instead of drawing a paycheck, things ran like a Swiss watch."

Lupe said, "Once you get him going, there's no stopping him— though, Rosalinda has to work to get him going every now and then."

"Well, he was certainly going this week," I said. "All I could do was be impressed."

Chuy obviously knew enough about the process to venture a guess. "So did you get about a third of what you need?"

I answered, "Yes, four of the twelve thousand needed. My feet are worn out from stomping all that mud."

They both laughed at the image of me doing it the "old fashioned" way. Lupe said, "I guess Rosalinda and I should have helped you in the mud pit."

Chuy said, "I wanna picture of that." Then he offered, "You're probably hungry and too tired to cook after the long week. Why don't we run up to the Slo Poke Cafe for dinner? They'll be busy, but I doubt we'd have to wait too long for a table."

"That sounds a lot better than the peanut butter and pickle supper I was planning to have," I said. "I'm ready when you are."

"Well, let's go," Lupe said.

We were in luck. There was an empty booth Alicia was just wiping down. At one of the larger tables was Bill, Betsy, Brett and several unknowns—one woman clearly about Brett's age but who looked a little older to my reckoning and four children in a sliding range of barely teenage to barely school age.

I said to my companions, "Girlfriend or wife, do you think?"

Lupe said, "I have no idea."

Then Chuy said, "His kids or hers or both, do you think?"

Lupe said, "Why you asking me? Your guess is as good as mine." But then a second later she said, "You can see that oldest boy is his—looks just like Brett did when he was that age."

Chuy confirmed, "He sure does. That next girl has some Geermann in her too if I'm seeing correctly."

We tried to mind our own business, which wasn't easy when the best entertainment was only a few feet away. Bill saw us and knew we were curious. Since I'd met Brett out at the ranch, and since Chuy and Lupe both knew him even though they'd not seen him in several years, Bill didn't bring him over for common courtesies. Instead he came by himself and sat next to me in the booth.

"I know you're wondering," he started out. "All four are our grandchildren and all we know about. I'm not saying other children may not be out there we don't know about. The two oldest are from his ex-wife in Odessa who still has primary custody so we don't see the kids much. The other two are from two different women in El Paso, and the woman with him here today he says he's gonna marry when they can get around to it. I told him earlier today, he could drive to Ojinaga today and get married, but he didn't get up off the couch. She has three kids of her own, who are with her two ex-husbands this weekend. What a mess. Grandchildren in the next generation are going to be mighty confused if they ever want to work on their family tree. Well, I'd better get back to the circus."

With that he was back up to rejoin the family. I thought maybe he'd ask about the work this week, but he didn't bother. I suppose with family on his mind, the little progress made the first week might have paled in comparison.

As they prepared to leave, Betsy stopped at the table to say hello. The youngest, a boy, was walking with her holding her hand. He had a pleasant little smile and seemed well behaved and fond of his grandmother. Lupe commented as much.

Betsy said, "Would you believe this is the first time we've ever been with him? We knew he existed but when we'd try to see him in El Paso there was always some reason it wouldn't work."

We all read that as the mother wouldn't accommodate their request but not wanting to say it so directly in front of the boy.

Then she asked me, "How's the adobe coming along?"

"Very good," I said. "We've made a third of what we need and will press on Monday and as long as the weather holds."

"Bill will be excited," she said. "Y'all have a nice dinner."

"Take care, Ms. Schlatter," I replied.

As is my habit of taking stock of the aftermath of any large or noisy table in a restaurant, I looked over to the Schlatter table now empty of people and still full of plates and glasses. I said to my companions, "Looks like Betsy ensures good manners in public even with children she's met for the first time. That table looks like everyone just left the Sunday dinner table."

Chuy said, "I'm sure Brett set some ground rules before they arrived. He knows what's expected of him and his kids."

Lupe said, "I have more than an inkling from the looks of the bunch he's a lot better father than he ever has been a husband."

I said, "There are plenty who are neither good husband nor good father. When my life was all failure, I at least had the consolation of my failures being my own and not burdened upon the innocent."

Chuy said, "We've always had to take your word for it, and we know well enough how little you had when you came here. Still, it's hard to see you as the failure you've long described."

"I appreciate that," I said. "Maybe that means I was able not to transmit my despair to others—that's something I hoped I was able to do despite the desperation of the times."

As we visited over dinner that night, it seemed to me that even though my situation had changed, being part of their lives had not. I really did begin to feel like I was just another piece of the Cardona fabric, woven as it was throughout Fort Davis. Perhaps working now "for the family" strengthened that bond even more.

Chapter Twenty-two

Ernesto and Bill had agreed that every Friday morning, weather permitting, Bill and Betsy would meet us at the jobsite to be sure all was progressing satisfactorily. Bill was out at the ranch far more days than not, but those trips were to attend to the needs of the ranch and not to stand around watching us work. Some days we would see him and some not. He also said we could use the bunkhouse during the day for our *baño* and said he would let us know any time he or other ranch hands were staying overnight. Otherwise, if for any reason we wanted to stay over and save a trip back and forth into town, we were welcome to spend the night there as well.

Ernesto had told him, "If it looks like we have to work on the adobe to beat the snow flying, we'll probably take you up on that."

That was one thing that worried him about the schedule. While the late fall had provided the dry weather we needed to crank out all the adobes, their cure time put us that much closer to colder weather in getting them laid. Our day-to-day crew would consist only of me, Ernesto and Roberto. Manuel and Sergio would be brought in only as needed when more hands were necessary, such as when we did concrete pours or if Ernesto felt like we were falling behind.

Ernesto laid his plans out for Roberto and me. "The way that ridge is tucked in with those mountains to the west, we should get pretty good protection from the worst of the winds, but that exposure to the north over that ridge is going to bear down hard when a true norther blows in. We're going to stand up the north wall first, while the weather is still warm and get the windows and doors in so we at least give ourselves a decent windbreak. If we don't, our *bolitas* are going to freeze off.

"We'll be laying a good two hundred and fifty adobes a day if we keep humping it, so that gives us two months to get the walls stood up on all three buildings."

"Damn!" was all Roberto said.

"What's wrong, *muchacha*? Don't think we can do it?" Ernesto asked.

"No problem, *jefe*," Roberto replied.

"That's more like it," Ernesto said.

For me it was all information to digest as we went along. I certainly had no notion as to the degree of effort all this would take, but since I'm pretty good with math in my head, it didn't take me long to work out those two months of adobe laying meant working every Saturday. I'd already gathered from Roberto and what I knew of Ernesto's schedule from our lunches at the Slo Poke Cafe twice a month on Saturday, that he was certainly working to beat the weather on this job. I suspect it was Roberto's realization that he'd be working every Saturday that brought about the exclamation.

Ernesto and Bill worked together on the bill of materials for the big-ticket items, and Bill would see to getting those ordered. Betsy was already spec'ing out the appliances she wanted. Once we got all the footers dug, Ernesto loaded up the John Deere on his lowboy trailer to take it over to a ranch on Limpia Creek where he always got his river rock. A lot of the rock over the years he got for free in exchange for various jobs on the ranch including rock and adobe work.

Ernesto said, "Every year we think we're about done with getting river rock from the ranch, and every year a good gully-washer opens up a whole new supply. Of course, if it does run out, Davis Mountain rock is pretty too, but I know Bill wants river rock if we can get it."

He'd already made arrangements with the ranch to start hauling what we'd need. He was going to leave the tractor there long enough for his brother, Mando, to haul the rock out to the ranch in his dump truck.

Once they were cured, with every trip to the ranch we'd haul more adobes on the lowboy. Ernesto had heavy tarps, and any night when he thought it would even be chilly he'd say, "Cover 'em up tonight boys. I don't want 'em catching a cold."

First thing when the sun would come out, we'd uncover them to warm up. It was the same for the walls so long as they were still going up. I guess it worked. The couple nights it did get to freezing while we were laying the walls, none ever froze enough to loosen the mortar from the block.

About once a week, Sallie would ride over to take a look. She rarely got off her horse or said a word. She'd sit up there in the saddle, look at the progress for about five minutes and ride towards home. Our Friday morning weekly briefings with Bill and Betsy sometimes included Jean and Mary-Alice. Brett was back in El Paso —still courting his latest. Still, no sign of Billy.

Chapter Twenty-three

We had worked nonstop, six days a week without a single break from bad weather since the Monday I started in September—not to mention the couple Sundays. We had the adobes done. On the Friday before Thanksgiving week, Ernesto kidded Betsy, "See, you can be in by Christmas after all. Put your tree right over there by the window looking out over that ridge, sit here right next to where the fireplace will go and sing "Jingle Bells." It might be a little drafty without a roof but you didn't say it had to be done—just that you were in by Christmas."

Betsy just smiled and walked room-to-room enjoying the view from each. As she did every Friday, she'd spend a few minutes by herself in the chapel as it came slowly up from the ground.

Ernesto had not said what his plans were for us during Thanksgiving week. I think Roberto, like me, was afraid to ask. On that Friday briefing Bill said to us, "I don't expect to see you three out here at all next week. You've earned some time off. And whatever you're doing for Thanksgiving dinner is on us. Betsy's made arrangements with the Thriftway for you to get your meat and all the fixin's."

Ernesto said, "She didn't need to do that."

Bill said, "It had nothing to do with needin' to and everything to do with wantin' to. Let her do it."

She was in the chapel by then, and he smiled and added, "Generosity is one of her newer gifts. Don't thwart it. Up until now the only thing that benefited from her checkbook other than the department stores has been that church of hers. They've learned in short order that one of their members going over to the devil makes for hell on their operating budget."

Ernesto, Roberto and I smiled as we could see how Bill took real delight in that last part.

I was glad to have some days off, but knew I'd also be eager to get back to building. Ernesto and Roberto both had been patient, instructive teachers to the "greenhorn," as Ernesto referred to me in the early days. Now I could anticipate what either one of them needed, was strong enough to lug around anything and everything, and taking my lead from Ernesto, ate mostly fatty meat to stay satiated throughout the workday.

Over the years, I had pinched and saved until I now had enough I could trade in the Ranger. I couldn't afford anything new, but I was ready to go shopping while I had the free days. On Monday, I drove over to Fort Stockton and found a relatively new Ford F-150. They offered me $500 on the Ranger, which I knew was their little game to make me feel like I got something for it, while the cash deal without it probably would have yielded the same bottom line. At least now I had something with under fifty-thousand miles, and I drove from the dealer straight to Alpine in my new wheels.

I wanted to finally get to the bookstore to see if they had the book that had brought about such a transformation in Betsy. I'd forgotten the author's name, but relating as I did to its title, I didn't forget that.

I asked the store owner, "Do you have any copies in stock of *The Body Broken*?"

She said, "That sure has been a popular book in these parts. First, the Episcopal priest ordered fifteen copies for their book group. Then after they read it, they ordered another twenty to give to other people. Yes, I have three still in stock."

She walked me to them and handed me a copy. I was surprised it was a pretty short book. Then she picked up another much bigger book and said, "This is what they are reading now. Did you want a copy of it as well?"

"Sure," I said. "I need some things to read this week. In fact, I'll take two copies." So I also left the store with *Amazing Grace* by Kathleen Norris—one for me and one I thought I'd give to Betsy.

Ernesto and Rosalinda were expecting all their kids over for Thanksgiving and included Chuy, Lupe and me to join them. Still, I did stop in the Thriftway to get a few things from Betsy's holiday gift. I was just coming out of the grocery store with my sack of free groceries as she was headed in. I thanked her for the gift and she looked into the bag.

She said, "You could have done better than that! That's pretty skimpy."

I said, "I expect Rosalinda's shopping will make up for my lighter bag. I'm joining them for Thanksgiving dinner."

"Oh, okay then," she said.

Then I said, "If you will follow me to my truck I have something for you."

I set the grocery sack down on the front seat and grabbed the book. "I was in Alpine earlier to get a copy of *The Body Broken*. The owner said that the Marfa book group was reading this book. I bought one for myself and one for you. I looks interesting, and I thought if you already had a copy you could just give this one away."

She looked at it and said, "I don't have it. I look forward to reading it very much. Thank you."

We wished each other a happy Thanksgiving, and I was soon back home digging into Mr. Benson's book.

I loved the book. It was clear to me Mr. Benson was a gentle soul trying to lead wounded people back to some semblance of health—a broken church to greater unity. It also confirmed two other things for me—my obliviousness to Christianity as a whole and my long-held indifference, or perhaps suspicion is the better word, to its most zealous adherents.

With less to recover from, I didn't feel the need to read it a second time as Betsy had upon her first reading. I could easily see now how it brought about such a sudden change in her. I moved right on to the second book. With its subtitle, *A Vocabulary of Faith*, I hoped it would deliver on that score as I still felt like I had no common language with which to understand matters of the Christian faith—or any belief system for that matter. Merton had helped start that journey for me, but even after the few years I'd been digesting his words, the Catholic faith was still more foreign than familiar to me. I needed more perspectives to help guide me along the journey. Benson and Norris seemed to be the right guides for my next steps.

Thanksgiving day arrived and for the first time ever, I offered to drive someone else somewhere. Chuy and Lupe were going to ride with me in my new, used F-150. Since they didn't have any children, I was never really comfortable bringing up other people's children around them. I don't know that it would have bothered them—I just wasn't comfortable doing it. Once I started working with Ernesto, we were so focused on the weather and getting those adobes laid before the snow flew that we talked about little else but the normal "cutting up" workers do to keep themselves amused. We avoided politics unless it amused us and religion unless it amused us. We really never talked about family.

I realized as the day approached how ignorant I was of Ernesto and Rosalinda's children. I suppose they might have been at the big Easter gathering that I attended every year, but if they were, I didn't know who belonged to whom.

As we left the house to head over to dinner, I basically idled my way there to give me some time to get a little information on who would be there.

I said, "Fill me in on Ernesto and Rosalinda's kids. I don't know anything about them except there are two boys and three girls."

Chuy replied, "*Un chico, tres chicas, un chico*. The oldest, Tomás, lives and works in the oil fields around San Angelo. He's married, wife is Margareta, and has two girls and two boys—all of whom have Lupe's quilts, of course. The next oldest is Berta. She is in San Angelo as well. She went to school there and now teaches in the public school. Married to Martin, two kids—*una chica, un chico*. I think she is pregnant again. The next younger girl is Conchita."

Lupe interrupted, "I never liked that name."

Which prompted Chuy to repeat it, "Conchita goes to the university part-time in San Angelo now and lives with her sister Berta, despite Martin wishing such was not the case. She appears to be aiming at becoming a perpetual student. The youngest girl is Tex."

Lupe jumped in, "That's not her real name. Ernesto calls her that sometimes because he says the doctor thought they were having another boy. Her proper name is Maria."

Chuy was feeling playful, "Tex lives in Fort Stockton with her husband, Bobbie, and they have one kid with another on the way.

"Three marriages and no divorces—so far.

"And the baby of the family is *Jesus Alexandro Pablo Cardona*— yes, you guessed it, Chuy for short—named after me if you can believe it. I guess because of that, he turned out the best."

"He would put it that way," Lupe said to me.

Chuy continued, "To Ernesto's shock, in high school he announced he was going to be a priest. He's off in seminary and should finish this spring. Then he plans to do at least a year's missionary work somewhere in Central America. Who knows after that—I'm thinking before I die, Pope Chuy the First.

"You've puttered along in these new wheels of yours just slow enough for me to get in what you need to know for now. This will be the first time all of them have been home all at once in several years. It's the first time for Chuy to be home since he left for seminary."

Ernesto was out in his carport when we arrived deep-frying two big turkeys. He said, "*Jaime,* If you want a good moist turkey, forget the oven. This is the only way to cook 'em."

Inside, the house was crowded with children and grandchildren. Rosalinda and her daughters were just waiting for the green light from Ernesto to start pulling things out of the oven and refrigerator—to set on the long table Ernesto had made soon after they were married.

Rosalinda said, "I knew when I saw him working on that table he expected me to have a dozen kids. I said, 'Forget it! You'll have to wait for your grandchildren before you see that table filled with your own family.' As you can see, nowadays it's full when everyone is here."

As we prepared to eat, Ernesto toasted Betsy and Bill as "the founders of the feast," which they indeed were. Those who were able to stay awake watched football on their satellite TV. I've just never been a sports fan, so I sat back quietly keeping to myself—almost invisible to everyone there, which suited me fine—as I watched the dynamics of this somewhat scattered, and diverse in its own way, wing of the Cardona clan. In a day or two, they'd be back to their own lives, and I'd be back to working on the ranch.

Chapter Twenty-four

Back on the job, Ernesto had lined up Manuel and Sergio to work with us until the roofs were on. He let Roberto take the lead on that, as he was a good carpenter. Ernesto wanted to get the fireplace and chimney going, for which he knew again we would have to watch for any deep freezes headed our way. I was to tend for him, which meant mixing mud and lugging around a lot of rock, fire brick and flue pipes as needed. We had conferred with Bill and Betsy about the final details on the look of the fireplace and wood box on the Friday before Thanksgiving.

Ernesto made it plain from the start that none of us on the crew were to ever bring up notions of when we might be done. As he put it, "I don't want to jinx anything—I don't want any bragging about how good things are coming along." While I wanted to commend him for how well both he and Bill were managing the flow of all the work, I let it be.

He was about four feet up the face of the fireplace one afternoon as he kept rolling around the rock pile that I kept stocked inside, looking for just the right rock. I spotted one I thought looked right and handed it to him. He placed it up in the spot and hollered for the other men to hear, "Who knew this *pendejo* could pick just the right rock!"

Not everyone can use the word *pendejo* as a term of endearment, but I had to smile at him, knowing it was, as I said to him, "Better a *pendejo* than a *cabrón*."

He asked, "You calling me a *cabrón*?"

"Only if the shoe fits," I said.

He said, "Rosalinda says it does, but what does she know!"

Somehow that put him in a singing mood and he broke into full voice singing one of his favorite Mexican folk songs and then another and then another before he finally hollered, "*Es todo por hoy, muchachas!*"

We tidied up for the day, and as we'd planned—spent that night and every other night that week at the bunkhouse, still doing what we could to stay ahead of any real winter that might come our way. We took Sunday off and made plans to repeat the same for the coming week. Ernesto wanted those roofs on and that chimney done.

He and I were taking down the scaffolding on the second Friday just as Bill and Betsy were driving in along with Jean and Mary-Alice following right behind. None of them had made it out the Friday before so they'd not seen anything in the works on either the roofs or the fireplace. As soon as we got back down off the roof, Ernesto greeted them and then went in to build a very tiny fire in the still curing fireplace. "We start small with a masonry fireplace," he instructed, "but it's good to get little fires going—let them burn out and then have another little fire."

Betsy was beaming. "Not only can I put my little Christmas tree up, I can even build me a little fire."

Before Thanksgiving, Ernesto had told Roberto and me that he'd scheduled the roofers to come do the standing seam steel the third week of December. I thought surely we'd be moving that out to after Christmas, but by damn, we were ready. While he confided in us his intent to have the roof done by Christmas, he had not said anything to Bill. Bill had already given the roofers the order for exactly what he and Betsy wanted so it would be in stock when the time came.

Bill said, "Looks like we can get the steel guys out here right after the holidays. You want me to give them a call?"

Ernesto said, "I've already called them. They say they'll be out here Monday. We'll see. I'll let you know if they don't show up." Then he added, "We're ready for the electrician to get crackin' again too. He's supposed to be out here Monday as well."

"Well, Betsy will be thrilled," he said. She and the girls had gone out to her beloved chapel.

"Bill, one other thing," Ernesto said. "It's time to think about cabinets. Are you going to go with stock made or get a cabinetmaker? Either way we ought to decide and get them spec'ed out and on order."

Bill said, "I think what we'll do is go to Home Depot and Lowe's in El Paso and check things out. I'm not sure who around here I'd want to trust to build something nice unless you know of someone I don't. The only good cabinet shop we had moved to Midland. I've seen the work from a couple others who call themselves custom cabinetmakers, but I wouldn't put their work in the bunkhouse.

"Besides, we'll be halfway to El Paso anyway. We're going to Van Horn to have lunch with Billy on Tuesday. It will be the first time his mother's seen him since he was sixteen. Damn, that's been twenty years ago already." He laughed adding, "I've seen some over the years so at least I'll recognize him when he walks in the restaurant." He chuckled again, "We'll see if his mother does."

I thought part of me understood the laugh and part of me didn't. I would learn later it was a funnier comment than we workers could understand at the time.

Wednesday was our last day to work before Christmas. Bill and Betsy said they wanted to do a lunch for us at the new house that day. We cleaned up after the electrician, the plumber—who had shown up that week to do a little more of his work—and all our mess. As instructed by Betsy, Ernesto had invited Manuel, Sergio, Mando and Rogelio out to the shindig, and without Betsy knowing it we set up a ten foot tree in the great room, had lights on it run from a long extension cord and had a small fire going in the fireplace by the time they arrived. It was a full family affair. Bill had told us that Brett, along with his "now wife" and his four kids, would be staying in the bunkhouse over the holidays. They were the first to show up at the house. As usual the girls arrived with Bill and Betsy. This time there was one new face in the crowd.

When Bill had announced they were meeting Billy in Van Horn, I'd asked Ernesto what he remembered of Billy. He said, "The boy took off so quick I'd never paid enough attention to him to know anything about him. I wouldn't know him if I saw him."

I was standing across the room next to Ernesto. He said without moving his lips, "Well, holy shit!"

That exclamation was all I needed to confirm what I already knew—it was Billy. And he was not in least bit what I expected. He looked nothing like the tall, lanky Bill. Bill, with his somewhat angular face, thinning brown hair slowly turning gray, and bright hazel eyes bore no physical resemblance to this young man in the least.

Billy was short—maybe five-eight, five-nine tops, and he was stocky with shoulders so wide it almost looked like he had on football shoulder pads. He looked like a small tank or a brick shithouse—not sure which is the more suitable analogy. His hair was thick and almost jet-black. He had large obsidian eyes.

One thing Bill, Ernesto and I have in common is possessing no butt. Our jeans sag in the back—our backside a near straight line from our tailbone to the back of our legs. Any straight man would have to notice that Billy had the ass of a professional dancer—packed into his wrangler jeans. Any tighter and he'd have to have them custom-made. Ernesto either read my mind or had the same thought. He leaned to me and said, "With an ass like that Rosalinda would be saying, 'Umm, umm, umm!'"

Since seeing Billy was not that big a surprise, I soon figured out Ernesto's "Holy shit!" exclamation. He went over to greet Billy.

"You won't remember me, but I'm Ernesto Cardona. You'd have been just ahead of my oldest boy, Tomás in school. Holy shit, boy! When you walked in that door I thought your granddad had been raised from the dead! You are the spittin' image of him!"

Now, I got Bill's making light of his mother not recognizing him —he apparently looked exactly like her father.

Billy said, "I thought Mom was going to faint when she saw me. And yes, I do remember you and Rosalinda. Every kid growing up knew who badass Ernesto was. We all admired your ability to live life as you saw fit."

Ernesto said, "I didn't know I'd been a role model all these years. Rosalinda always said I was a bad influence. I'll have to set her straight."

Bill said to Billy, "As you can see, not much has changed on this end—still the same old character he was when you left."

Ernesto introduced us, his crew, as well as his brothers Mando and Rogelio—and then promptly commandeered the spirit of the crowd one more time as only a personality like Ernesto can. He broke into song as he sang both English and Spanish verses of "Oh Holy Night." It was so beautiful I had to turn away to hide the tears—and I wasn't the only one.

Chapter Twenty-five

Bill and Betsy didn't expect us to work between Christmas and New Year's, but Ernesto and Roberto both said they had houses full of family and would just as soon work and see family in the evening. I certainly had no objection, so the three of us pressed on, up to and including working until about four o'clock on New Year's Eve. Bill, Betsy and Billy came out to sit in the great room one sunny afternoon midweek and were surprised to find the three of us working away—no electrician or plumber in sight, though both were made aware we'd be around if they showed up to work. Neither said they had plans not to work and yet neither showed up to do any work.

Ernesto had a one word reaction, "Typical."

I expected *cabrón* to get worked in there at least, but it was clear this job was indeed inspiring him to clean up his act somewhat. That "holy shit" was the only thing close to profanity I'd ever heard him say in front of Betsy, and I speculated that when she saw Billy in the restaurant in Van Horn that first time after all those years, she probably said it or thought it herself.

Bill had told us some time back that he figured it was a long shot that they could ever get Billy to come work on the ranch, if for no other reason than Billy had a heck of a good deal on the ranch where he'd been working all these years. That ranch spread over two counties as compared to the several sections here, and Bill saw that as a step down too far for Billy to really see any future in it.

The little I knew about Schlatter finances mostly came from Chuy. He said that Bill came into the marriage with a pretty healthy income himself. His family had oil and gas rights scattered from San Angelo to Midland, and in boom years Bill got plenty to set aside for those bust years in between. Bill loved the ranch far more than the oil fields, but as Chuy reckoned it, the oil fields were building the new house and would pay the salary for Billy to run the ranch if he ever did come home to work. All the ranch had to do was hang on so long as the oil money lasted, and Chuy figured, too, that Sallie would leave her ranch to Billy if he came home—

giving him a shot at having a big enough ranch "to make a livin' if not a killin'" as Chuy put it.

Seeing we were there, Bill had brought in with him from the truck a folder with colored brochures and detailed order sheets for all the bathroom, office and kitchen cabinets.

"Now I've not ordered these yet, boys," he clearly directed to Ernesto and me. "I wanted you two to look them over carefully to be sure we've got everything right. If we do, all I have to do is call and tell them to run with it. If it's wrong, mark it up to what it ought to be."

"Will do," Ernesto said.

Billy with his parents strolled around the house and spent some time back in what we'd envisioned as "Billy's wing." Betsy announced she was going to her chapel for a few minutes, and Billy asked if he could join her.

"Well, of course, son," was all she said.

Then Bill took that opportunity to share the news with us. "When I asked Billy if he'd ever leave his good job to work for pinto beans on a two-bit ranch he said, 'Dad, I see just how much big ranches like the one I'm at are little more than a plaything for their rich owners. I don't like workin' there. They pay enough, but I know they could, and most likely will, sometime walk away and not give a shit about what's left behind. For them, they'd just as soon get rid of all the cattle and call it a wildlife preserve where they'd get a complete tax exemption, taking that bit of income from the counties. And you and I both know you need a healthy stand of ruminants on the grass to keep it healthy. In ten years, their preserve would be just more desolate West Texas sand blowing with every passing storm. I'd quit in a heart beat.' I said, 'Then quit and come home. We've built rooms for you in the new house.' And he said, 'When it's done, I'll be there.'"

Bill said, "When I heard those words, I never hugged a boy so hard in all my life, and I couldn't let go."

Chapter Twenty-six

After the Schlatters had gone, Ernesto went out to his truck, away from the noise of Roberto and me setting doors and trim, to look over the cabinet order carefully. He didn't spot anything that needed changing and asked me to go over them carefully that evening when I got home. If it looked good, we'd call Bill first thing in the morning and tell him to get them ordered.

Ernesto said, "I'd tell you to call him tonight, but I'm sure you still don't have a phone."

I said, "I can get free phone service from you and Chuy if I really need it." Then I said, "I hope these don't take a day longer than the estimated lead time or we're going to wish we'd ordered them a couple weeks earlier."

Ernesto said, "I saw that too. I'm kicking myself for not getting that going earlier. *Soy un pendejo.*"

"Not hardly," I said. "We've got plenty still to do. We might just have to work outside more than we planned right now."

We had a lot of stone columns to stand up. When we framed the porches, we used steel posts, which Ernesto likes to use and then rock around. We also had some rock walls inside in the foyer, and we were moving ahead with the rock wall around the chapel. Ernesto also wanted to lay some flagstone walks, which he, Bill and Betsy had one time marked out with orange spray paint. He would repaint it again when we were ready to start for Bill and Betsy to confirm one last time before becoming permanent.

Much to Ernesto's chagrin, Easter, while not the earliest possible date when it can fall, was close thereto. The cabinets would make or break being done by Easter.

We thought it was good news when Bill gave us the word the cabinets had shipped on time. However, the good news was short-lived when we heard that the cold front that brought heavy snow to the mountains and ice on I-10 had caused a pileup involving the semi transporting the cabinets. Thankfully, no one was killed—but it took three days before the truck line could check the load to see what survived and what was lost in the wreck. They wanted us to come check, piece by piece, as it was moved off the trailer. Bill,

Ernesto and I went to see how bad it was. Bill kept the checklist as we went over each piece and tallied room by room. There were a few that needed just some minor touch-up, which we agreed should be released as okay to deliver as is. There were several beyond any repair.

Bill said, "We couldn't have gotten any luckier. It's just my office cabinets and shelves that we'll have to reorder. I can work off a card table. At least we can get that house done and Billy home." Then Bill said, "You boys may not realize it, but the Eastern Orthodox celebrate Easter later than the Protestants and Catholics. We might just have to tell Betsy she should have been more specific."

Even on the Catholic calendar, Betsy, Bill and Billy were in by Easter. We continued to work on columns and walkways. Bill said he and Billy were going to try to forge and weld together a nice gate for the rock wall and soon-to-be rose garden. Ernesto had said just a day or two earlier that we needed to start thinking about what we were going to do about a gate. Now it seemed that was sorting itself out.

Then Bill said if we didn't have any other work lined up pressing on us, he'd like us to do some work on the bunkhouse. "We need to freshen up the outside of that since we now drive by it every time we—or anyone else—comes and goes, and inside I want to get it better-suited for Brett and his family when they come to visit."

The same morning we were finishing up the flagstone, Bill and Billy arrived with their creation in the back of the pickup.

Ernesto saw what they were carrying and after he got past his initial, "Damn, that looks real nice," he said. "Roberto, you go see if they need any help. They probably will be trying to figure out how to hang it from the rock wall. I don't want 'em knocking my rocks loose."

I thought of a thing or two I could say to that last part, but was busy enough I didn't bother.

When we laid the last flagstone and were going to head over to get started on the bunkhouse, Bill handed Ernesto an envelope. With it he said, "Here ya go. One title to a John Deere tractor." Then he handed me, Roberto and Ernesto another envelope.

"Ernesto, I didn't think it's quite right to buy you a new pickup since these other two helped get us over the finish line. Here's our thank-you for a job well done."

It seemed all three of us lacked the courage to open the envelopes in front of him. We did manage to mutter a rather shocked, if pathetic, "thank you", which I suspect was about all he expected at that moment anyway.

In the truck heading home, we couldn't help but compare since he'd not said we couldn't. They were almost all the same—$10,000, except mine included $500 more. Ernesto laughed, "They got that $500 to you after all for staying up all night working on those plans!"

It had been seven months since we made the first adobes. I asked Ernesto if this was typical or not.

He said, "In the big cities, they can build them in half the time. Of course, they are stick building and don't have to make their own bricks. Out here, seven months would be considered miraculous to most. I've seen projects drag on for three or four years. I'm there to build, not to homestead."

Part III

Chapter Twenty-seven

I thought my life with the Schlatters would wind down now that the house was done. We had a few weeks work to do on the bunkhouse, and I thought that might well be the last time I'd ever be out on the ranch. While they had told a number of people who had seen the house and liked it very much that I had drawn it for them, no one came clamoring for house-rendition services. Ernesto really wanted me to get a computer with some CAD software so that we could offer some design services along with his construction. He put his $10,000 back into the business with a new truck, and I decided I should abide his request and get the computer and software.

While we worked on the bunkhouse, Billy came by every day. I think because he left so young, he didn't feel any connection to other men still around who he would have known in his school days. Most of them had moved away and those who stayed were married with families. This led to a rather natural association with me since we were basically the same age and neither of us had ever married. Ernesto interrupted his folk-song serenade one day to announce to Billy that I played the guitar and sang—even suggesting I could improvise my own tunes. I guess Chuy or Lupe had mentioned it somewhere along the line. We'd never talked about it. How he pulled that out of the clear blue was a mystery to me—the spirit moving perhaps as it had when I stood on that ridge and envisioned the house now standing there.

Billy said, "Maybe you can compose some tunes to go with my dad's lyrics or poems or whatever they are called. I play the fiddle and harmonica some, but I've never been able to set his words to music."

I said, "Well, I am a novice at best, and with the work of this past year I'm pretty sorry on practice time. Still, I'd love to see some of your dad's writings if he'd share them."

I found myself staring at Billy way more than I should. I couldn't help my mind trying to wrap itself around how this fine, handsome man—so charismatic in my mind for a cowboy—and his mother could have become so alienated from each other for twenty years. And how if it were not for one woman giving his mother a book, how the alienation might have remained for the rest of their lives. This was at once a weight and sadness, and yet redeemed in the moment of those heavy feelings. I recalled often his dad's words when Billy said he'd come back home.

"I never hugged a boy so hard in all my life, and I couldn't let go."

He's not my son or brother, but perhaps because I never had any such hug from father, brother, mother or sister, I seemed to long for such an embrace somehow now with this lost sheep safely back in the fold—clearly no worse for wear and with a heart that seemed as big as those broad shoulders settled above it. I longed too for a friend my age—someone to confide in. As much as I was part of the Cardonas now, in so many respects, I was still outside looking in. I was the friend to be included, which I was in all the most positive aspects of the word. But what would happen if I moved from the casita at some point? Would I still be close to Chuy and Lupe in any proximity to how close we were now? When Ernesto retired or if something happened to him, what would my life look like then?

These kinds of questions, at their core, were not allowing me to take the days as they came as I had done so well for so long. I realized this, but at the same time I was nagged by the fact that somehow Billy represented another chapter in my life. I just couldn't align any reasonable conclusion around this nagging. His suggestion now that I try to write some tunes for his dad's words seemed like some door he, too, was trying to put his foot into just in case it meant something. I don't think either one of us was steady on our feet—not just yet.

It was Friday afternoon and we were packing up at the bunkhouse for the day. Billy suggested I come over to the house, "I don't have a guitar, but we do have a mandolin. Let's see how well we fit playing together."

Ernesto couldn't help himself. "Boys fittin' together to play. You two are full of surprises."

I said, "You tell him I play guitar and then twist the poor boy's words."

Ernesto retorted, "Hey, just sayin'—it is a Friday night."

Billy responded, "I'll take *Jaime* back to town later this evening. Maybe we can go to the Slo Poke Cafe. You and Rosalinda can chaperone if you're worried about our being seen in public together. You can keep an eye on us to be sure we behave."

I rode with Billy back to the house. It was my first time there since they'd all moved in. Billy had his own entrance on one end with french doors opening from his library/sitting room/kitchenette to the great room. While I expected to use his back door, he went straight in the front. Bill and Betsy weren't home. As natural as two junior high boys, he put his arm around my shoulder and led me through the great room and into his wing of the house. There he had his fiddle, the mandolin and his harmonica.

"Do you need music or do you play by ear?" he asked.

I said, "I've learned to read music by chords, which is to say I can play as good by ear as from most music scores. But if you're expecting anything approaching stage quality, you need to lower your expectations about ten notches. I'm barely past beginner. I just know a few tunes I can sing from memory."

Billy got his fiddle and harmonica poised for whichever he thought might fit best with his next request.

"Just pick a song and go for it," he said.

"I guess I should start with my new theme song. My old theme song is a story all its own and for another time perhaps."

So I got the feel of the mandolin more or less and started in on "Tumbling Tumbleweeds." With the first chorus, Billy joined in with his harmonica. I didn't even know I liked the harmonica! As I looked at him, and he at me, I was smiling brightly—and you could see the pleasure of the music in his expressive eyes as well. I let him take a "lick" of his own after the chorus before starting the second verse.

He had not closed the french doors from the great room and we suddenly had an audience with Bill and Betsy listening. When we finished, both applauded.

Betsy said, "I didn't know you could play and sing as well."

I said, "Fort Davis has meant a lot of firsts for me."

Then Billy said, "Dad, we want some of your lyrics and poems you've written. We'd like to see if we can get them and some music together."

Bill replied, "They're out in my office. I'll go grab a few."

Betsy said, "Jaime, I hope you'll stay for dinner. Bill is going to grill some ribeyes. I'm making a salad. Simple but delicious supper, if you will join us."

I didn't get a chance to answer before Billy said, "He'll stay."

"I guess I'm staying," I said. "Billy *is* my ride home."

She left with the parting order, "Make music, boys, but move it into the big room."

Billy said not too loudly, *"Jawohl, herr kommandant."* Then he said, "That's what we used to say to her when we were kids. Of course we got that from 'Hogan's Heroes.'"

From a distance we heard Betsy say, "I heard that!"

Bill was back with half a dozen scraps of paper each with a different title. I said, "These may be for just studying right now. Could be it will take some thought as to whether either of us can do anything with them since neither of us has ever done songwriting before."

Bill, quite matter-of-factly stated, "You never drew a house or built one before, and now you're sitting in it playing and singing."

He handed me a sheet with a piece he'd called, "Wall Street Banditos". He said, "It starts with the refrain."

I read through the lyrics and passed them to Billy. He said, "Oh, I remember this one when you showed it to me in Van Horn a few years back."

"I have a fondness for it," Bill said. He left the room for his favorite chair next to the fireplace.

Billy passed the lyrics back to me. It had such a simple rhythm a tune came right to me. I thought it probably belonged to some other song, but I started right in anyway. As soon as Billy caught on to the tune, he was looking over my shoulder singing along with great gusto.

Oh, the rich don't go to jail.
No, the rich don't go to jail.
No, the rich don't go to jail.
They go to the country club.

Poor Henry needed a home
and the bankers said, 'okay.'
Then they took the job away
leaving Henry alone in the fray.

(Refrain)

So the sheriff came along
and took his home to sell.
Said they, 'who gives a damn!
old Henry can go to hell.'

(Refrain)

When the agent went inside
he found a stash of weed.
And before he could even cry
They hauled Henry off for the deed.

(Refrain)

The judge sealed Henry's fate.
He was sure that weed was bad.
It was ruinin' his fine state.
And poor Henry's life was had.

(Refrain)

And you know this story's true.
Not a damn thing they will do.
For the poor they'll put the screw
And they'll damn sure screw you too.

Betsy hollered to Bill from the kitchen clearly intending for us to hear. "All the pretty things you've written, and you had to give them that one first! Come get these steaks on. Your grill's been hot for ten minutes!"

Billy said, "This time, I'll add the fiddle," and we were off for a replay of "Wall Street Banditos."

As we sat down to eat, Billy said, "I guess other than those cocktail meatballs at the Christmas luncheon, this is probably the first Geermann-Schlatter beef you've had."

"Well, yes, knowingly at least," I answered.

Bill said, "I didn't even think to ask how you might want it. We always eat 'em medium rare. Do I need to put yours back on the grill?"

I assured him, "No—just how I would have ordered it."

Betsy asked who would like to say a blessing. I found myself volunteering for the second time in my life and repeated the same blessing I had used at Chuy and Lupe's.

Let us taste no food that does not strengthen us to show thy great love and mercy. Amen.

They all repeated, "Amen." No sign of the cross before or after. I assumed that was a Catholic thing.

Betsy said, "What a lovely blessing."

So as to give proper credit where credit is due, I said, "It's adapted from a book I have by the late monk, Thomas Merton."

Bill said, "A few protestants who go on and on could learn from it. Dig in, boys."

We visited at the dining table for a long time before retiring to the living room to talk some more. Billy shared a goodly number of the encounters with his mega-rich employer and the people who would come to the ranch. As Billy said of most of them, "Apparently, I was supposed to know who they were and that they were really something. Pardon me Mother, but most of them were stuck-up, dumb shits who had a hissy fit if a little tarantula ran in front of them."

The time had gotten away from us. Bill looked at his watch and asked, "Jaime, what time do Chuy and Lupe go to bed on a Friday night?"

I said, "About the same every night. Right about 10:30."

Then he said, "I don't want Billy on roads this time of night with all the deer out and driving through the mountains. I'm gonna give 'em a call and tell 'em you're staying out here with us. I hope that's okay. I don't want them worrying about you any more than I'd wanna worry about both of you."

I didn't want to put the son who had just come home in danger, so I said, "Sure. I don't have to be anywhere early tomorrow."

So as not to impose more than I already had, I said, "Billy, can you drive me up to the bunkhouse? It's a bit of a walk from here."

Betsy said, "You are *not* sleeping in the bunkhouse. You know which room is made up for guests—you put it there. That's your room anytime you stay here with us."

Bill visited with Chuy for several minutes. When he returned, he said to me but intended for all to hear, "I believe they miss you not being around so much. He talked about how they'd sit in the yard and listen to you sing. I decided not to tell him we'd had the pleasure of that tonight, ourselves."

Then Bill said, "I'm off to bed."

"Me too," I said. "It's been a delightful evening. Thank you so much."

Back in "my" room I realized, other than the nights in the bunkhouse, this was the only other place I've spent the night except my casita. For a moment I stepped outside in the chilly night air— no moon—stars so thick the Milky Way looked almost superimposed by some mammoth technology. A new prayer came to me as I stared into the vast cosmos. I'd heard the first line of a children's prayer when Rosalinda put one of the little ones to bed early on that first Thanksgiving I was there. It came again into my mind.

Now I lay me down to sleep.
The night is dark.
The sky so deep.
Oh, gentle spirit bless this peace,

and in my death grant sweet release.

I stood there a moment longer before going back in and crawling into bed. Eyes open, looking at the ceiling I prayed that first prayer again with a line I'd added weeks earlier.

Thank you for this day, for the wonderful people you have brought into my life, and grant me a peaceful night.

Chapter Twenty-eight

With the big projects all done, Ernesto was eager not to work Saturdays for the foreseeable future. He got no resistance from Roberto and me on that score. This weekend I had planned to go to the food pantry on Saturday morning, but I hadn't planned on spending the night out at the ranch.

I slept like a log even though, without an alarm, I wake up early out of habit. With only yesterday's work clothes to wear, I thought I should at least take a quick shower. Billy obviously heard me up and about, and when I came out of the bathroom he had laid a clean pair of jeans, white socks and a shirt on the bed. Our builds are very similar, and I am only maybe an inch taller than him. Everything else I might have needed was already taken into account in the bathroom by the gentility of my host, Betsy, who thought of everything a guest might need.

As I dressed and glanced in the mirror, I mumbled to myself, grinning widely, "These jeans are gonna wonder what happened to that ass that regularly fills 'em out."

It was just going on seven. Everyone was up, coffee made. Betsy was frying some bacon and said, "You won't turn down breakfast will you, Jaime?"

"No ma'am. Very kind of you."

Billy said, "Dad'll be in for breakfast. He had to run something over to Sallie's that he forgot to put in the mailbox. He mentioned that you used to help at the food pantry. Is that today?"

"Yes, but it won't collapse if I'm not there."

Billy said, "I'd like to go. I'm really curious who, if anyone, I would actually recognize or who might recognize me."

I replied, "I gather from what Ernesto said, probably every old lady in town is going to think you're Mr. Geermann."

Betsy said, "Here one of you watch this bacon for a moment." And she was off to her bedroom. Just as quickly she was back with an 8 x 10 picture of her mother and dad.

All I could do was look at Billy and then the photo and then at Billy again. "That is amazing!" I exclaimed.

Betsy added, "Dad would have been right at Billy's age in that picture. Good looks run in the family, wouldn't you say?"

"Clearly," was all I said. I decided not to ask about her father's hind end.

Bill was soon back just as breakfast was ready. We sat down, and Betsy asked, "Could I hear that blessing again, Jaime?"

I gave a simple agreeing nod and repeated my Merton blessing.

Billy and I cleared and did the dishes. Bill, who had cut down quite a bit but hadn't quit smoking altogether, went outside for one his King Edwards. Betsy said, "I'm sure Sallie had one of her Swisher Sweets lit up—now he has to have a cigar."

I gathered up my work clothes, placed them in a grocery bag Betsy gave me, and Billy and I headed to town getting there well before most of the volunteers. I was glad. It gave me a chance to introduce Emma to Billy as well as just visit with her a bit as she scurried around getting everything ready. It had been weeks since I'd seen her.

Once all the volunteers were there, Emma had a chance to relax a bit. I asked her how Claude was doing. "Still a bean burrito, salad and hot tea every Saturday. Need I say more?"

Rosalinda had just come in and saw me and Billy. She pulled on my shirt sleeve to get me out of the earshot of the others. She just reached her face up to my ear and said, "Umm, umm, umm."

I smiled and said, "That husband of yours—until Billy came along, it never occurred to me he might have checked out my ass when we first met!"

"Oh, I can't *wait* to tell him that!" She responded.

She was most tickled all morning about our brief derrière exchange. Later she asked me if I had on a new shirt—she hadn't seen it before.

It must be said it was a much higher grade than I could generally afford. I wasn't sure what to say, so I just said, "Of a kind." If she didn't know what I meant by that, she didn't ask.

It is interesting what people do ask when they don't know anything about you really. As a single man, I can't say how many times people start with,

"Are you married?"

When that's a no, then they might ask,

"Do you have kids?"

When that is also a no, most people give up. Nothing of interest to talk about after that apparently. Once in a blue moon, one will press further.

"Do you live alone?"

This is *the* slippery slope question. If you are my age and answer in the affirmative, they wonder what's wrong with you. I think they go home and check the sex offender registry. If you answer no, then they want to know gender, sexual orientation and why, if straight, you aren't married.

Rosalinda's innocent question about my shirt had sent me into this daydream even as I carried bags out to clients' cars, wondering what questions they might like to ask me if they had the nerve.

Emma motioned for me to come her direction. As I did, she walked into the office and I followed. She said, "Shut the door."

I could see something was up. She said, "I haven't made this public yet. Claude knows—no one else. It was confirmed this week —I've got cancer. It's too soon to say to what extent but they don't think it's good."

I am terrible with such news. Coming from a family with no common courtesy, still having never even attended a funeral in my life, never loving and being loved by anyone for so long, I find myself at a complete loss for words. I never had the impression that Emma was any more of a hugger than I, a trait passed down I supposed from her rather critical, engineer father. The only thing in the moment I could think to do or say was, "Life certainly doesn't come with an assurance of an easy road, does it?"

I guess that was as good as anything I could have said, because she said, returning to her more cheerful self, "No guarantees but one hell of a ride!"

"Thanks for telling me," I said. "Ernesto might even give me a day off here and there if you need a ride somewhere or errands or whatever. I'll do anything I can."

She said, "It might be obvious or not, but I'd rather have your help than most anyone else I can think of. I appreciate it."

She got up heading back to the door, and as we entered the hallway, I did put my arm around her shoulder while no one was in our line of sight. She went back to her duties and me to mine.

Billy meanwhile was giving hugs to the vast majority of little old ladies as they came in. You could see from their smiles that my prediction was correct—that they, better than the younger crowd, would recognize the resemblance to his grandfather. They would grin widely and pat their hand on his cheek. He said later that even the ones who were in school with him—if they recognized him—never spoke.

After closing, Billy and I joined Ernesto and Rosalinda at the Slo Poke Cafe. I was still riding with Billy. Ernesto was already there, spread out in the booth as usual. He quickly saw he had to swing around to make room for his wife.

Ernesto said, "Billy, did they snag you in their pantry net?"

Billy answered, "For at least today they did."

Rosalinda said, "Every old lady there knew exactly who he was and hugged and kissed on him. He was a celebrity."

Then why she had to add this, I don't know, "Doesn't *Jaime* look nice in his new shirt?"

Ernesto knew the kind of clothes I wore. He studied it about two seconds and said with his brow slightly wrinkled, "Billy, isn't that the shirt you had on at the Christmas luncheon?"

I figured I might as well come clean. If I had with Rosalinda earlier, the shirt might not have come up at all. I said, "Yes, it's Billy's shirt. We got to playing music after work which led to Bill grilling steaks, and we talked so long Bill didn't want Billy driving late at night to bring me home."

As I talked, I was thinking at the same time how my quick response offered more control over the narrative than if I'd left it for Billy to answer—though, no doubt, his version would have been far more colorful.

Rosalinda said, "Now I get the 'of a kind' reference to the shirt."

I could already see Ernesto was going to enjoy this just a bit too much and wondered about how Billy would react. Ernesto said, "I never took you for someone who would sleep over on the first date."

"Very funny," I said.

Billy put his arm around my shoulder and pulled me tightly to him. With a big grin on his face he said, "Do you think I could do any better in this town than what I've got right here?"

Then he took his other hand and put it on my cheek moving my face back and forth as he said, "Look at this face. Isn't it cute? He's like a little puppy dog. Just adorable!"

He'd beaten Ernesto at his own game.

Rosalinda said, "You'd have beautiful children."

I waited for Ernesto to say, which he did not, surprisingly, "Yeah, one with an ass and one without."

If there was one of the four of us who knew to what extent Billy's fun was in jest, or to some degree serious, I knew three of us had no clue. Whether Billy himself knew, I had to wonder. Given the setting, he certainly didn't show any restraint. Anyone half-awake would have seen and heard him, and I knew for certain that Sara heard it. I thought her eyes were going to pop out! She's not easily shocked, it must be said, but he'd done just that—and she grinned every time she came to our table, which now seemed as often as possible.

There was no way our lunch that day was going to be anything but lighthearted. Still, I had the nagging realization of Emma's news on my mind, which was only reinforced by the fact that Claude sat across the room with the back of his head directly in my line of sight.

After lunch Billy finally drove me home. He wasn't sure where Chuy and Lupe lived so I directed him back down the dusty street to my casita. He stopped right in front of it and said, "The only dog that could live in there with you would be a Chihuahua, and even he'd have to give you warning if he was gonna turn around."

I said, "It's not quite that small."

He said, "Dad always called the bunkhouse the 'ramshackle.' I'm not sure what he'd call this. Has he ever seen it?"

I said, "He's not been here since I've been living here, but I'd have to guess he probably knows Fort Davis well enough to have it pretty clearly in his mind."

"I'll have to ask him," Billy said.

"Let me go change so I can give you back your clothes," which I said thinking that he'd stay in the truck while I did so. He did not.

"Okay," was all he said as he got out and followed me in.

I felt a little awkward changing with him in the room, though I shouldn't have. I took my clothes into my tiny little bathroom and changed in there with the door most of the way shut but not closed all the way so as to not look too paranoid. I folded the jeans and shirt on my bed and twisted the socks together, handed him the pile and thanked him. "I had a good time," I said.

"So did I," he said. "More than I have for long time. Why don't you bring your guitar out next Friday, and we'll work on some more songs together? We might even take a stab at another of Dad's lyrics. I'll check with Mom, but I'm sure she'll want you to stay for supper—and once you do that you know you'll have to spend the night, or they'll both be frettin' about you being on the roads late at night."

I said, "I don't have a phone for you to let me know, but I guess we will be out at the bunkhouse again this week working, so just let me know."

"I can do that!" he said and was out the door and on his way back to the ranch.

Chapter Twenty-nine

Bill and Betsy weren't quite sure what to do with the house in town. For now, it was just sitting empty, which neither one wanted. Nor did they really want to rent it out unless it was to someone they knew well and who would be a long-term renter. They couldn't foresee it being much more suitable in their "old age" than the ranch since Fort Davis doesn't really have any infrastructure for the aging. Even the Alpine hospital ends up sending anything serious to Midland-Odessa. They were closer to Midland-Odessa at the ranch than they would be in town.

They were in Fort Davis together one Friday morning to go to the Thriftway and saw Annie Jacobs' car in front of her real estate office. They had known Annie since she moved there twenty years earlier, and always thought they would give her their business if they ever bought or sold anything. She was in the office by herself.

Bill said, "We're thinking of listing the house in town. Would two-seventy-five be anywhere in the ballpark?"

She replied, "I think that's right on the money, but you might not have to list it. I've got two men from Dallas who have been looking for a house in town. I drove them by your place last time they were out here and said there was a possibility it might be coming on the market. They liked it a lot from the outside. I know it's right in the sweet spot of what they want to spend."

Betsy asked, "You think they're really contenders for buying out here or just curious?"

Annie assured them, "Oh, they are serious. They come out here several times a year. Both aren't far from retirement, and they definitely plan to move here full-time when they do. They seem like really down-to-earth guys. You might have seen them in town sometime. If you saw two men in a black Jaguar—that was them."

Bill noted, "That black Jag will be hard to keep clean with the dust in Fort Davis, and I don't think they'll find anyone to work on it, but I guess they'll work that out without my help."

Annie said, "If they go for it, I'll just do three percent as my commission instead of the usual six percent."

Bill said, "Do you know if this would be a cash deal or would they be borrowing? The only reason I ask is, if you thought they'd be creditworthy, we could carry the note for ten to fifteen years at four percent."

Annie said, "I'm not sure if they'd be paying cash or not. We'd not gotten that far. Let me try to call them now just to see if they're as interested as I think they will be."

She picked up the phone and called them. Bill and Betsy heard only her half of the conversation. "John, it's Annie Jacobs. That house I drove you past last time you were out here—the one on Front Street—looks like it will indeed be coming on the market.... Yes, its right in your budget. Looks like it will be listed at two-seventy-five. I can go by this afternoon and take some shots inside and email some pictures to you...." She put her palm over the receiver and said to Bill and Betsy, "He said hang on...." "Oh! Sure. Yes, 10:00 works fine for me. Okay. I'll meet you at the house. Have a safe trip. Right, bye."

She hung up. "Well, I'd say they are serious. He said they are heading this way. I'm to meet them tomorrow morning—as you heard at 10:00."

Betsy said, "Yes, I'd say they're serious. I hope we are, too!" She said this realizing how quickly they went from a causal drop-in to possibly selling their long-time home.

Bill said, "Just give us a call when you have some news one way or the other. And keep the owner-financing option in mind. I'd rather do that than wait for them to get a mortgage approved out here, and I doubt they can do any better than four percent these days."

With that he handed her the keys.

The next day, it was after 2:00 when Annie finally called. "I bet you thought I had forgotten about you. We spent a long time at the house and then spent an even longer time visiting over lunch. They want the house and will pay the asking price. They'd love to finance half of it over ten years. If that all sounds good to you, I will get all the paperwork done and get their signatures on the contract this afternoon—both are sitting here in my office right now waiting for the green light."

Bill said simply, "The light is green."

Annie, doing her due diligence asked, "Is Betsy's light green as well?"

Bill laughed and said, "She assured me last night and again this morning—all green lights from this end."

"Great!" And with that Annie hung up to get busy on the sale.

Besty, Billy and I had huddled nearby. It had been another Friday night sleepover for me—something I had begun to think might become far more frequent than not.

When Bill hung up he said to Betsy, "Well, Mother, looks like you're going to be stuck out here with us from now on."

Betsy said, "I can't think of a lovelier thought. I'm going to go sit in the chapel for a while if any care to join me."

Bill said, "I think I'll have a King Edward out in my rocker, but maybe the boys will join you."

I think Billy thought the same as me. That that was a hint to let Bill be by himself, so we followed Betsy into the chapel.

Chapter Thirty

It would be hard for me to say who loved the chapel more—me or Betsy. While small, there was something about it that I was drawn to, and I know she was, too. I knew that a day didn't pass without her spending time in it. Of course, I could only spend time in there through my imagination, which I did often enough. This was really the first time I had the invitation and opportunity to join her and just sit in the silence of the place. We each took a seat next to the stair-stepped window wall so that each could look out to the east. When next to the window, you felt like you were in there alone, since you couldn't see the person sitting against the next window. From any window you had the view into the now-maturing rose garden with its many varieties of prolific—almost wild-looking bushes. You could see the rich colors of the perfectly, close-fit rock wall that Ernesto had laid up with all his skill—an act of love, as I always thought of his work. Past the wall lay the grass and the mountains under the vast skies that define the very character of the place. It was altogether lovely and nurturing.

I found my eye focused on one small oak tree up on the closest rise. It was barely a tree as trees go in much of the world. Here in the cleft of the rock upon which it grew, it clung to its difficult existence. The winds had forced its modest growth to bend eastward. To me, in that moment, it represented the struggles in life and how they shape us, how dependent we are on roots to keep us grounded against the forces wanting to blow us asunder—and how this oak represented what I was becoming, rather than the tumbleweed I had been that was so easily broken by the assailing winds in my life. That humble little oak gave me a wellspring of hope no sermon or pious words ever could. I felt myself moving from the *dreams* of a hopeful life to what it was fast becoming—a life of *abundance*. Not in some material sense—the desert makes no such offers. It was the deep silence within this simple chapel feeding me—as the world outside continued its own transformation —and any who allowed themselves to be transformed by it.

I don't know how long we were in there. It seemed as long as Betsy sat quietly there, Billy and I would, too. Neither of us got up to leave until she did. We went straight back to the house while she wandered in her rose garden for a bit. All three of us had spent part of our morning there deadheading and snatching up any little shoot that wasn't attached to a rose bush.

Billy and I settled in the rocking chairs on the ridge side of the porch. Bill was still on the south porch, where he could see his grass and cattle.

Betsy joined the two us briefly before going to join her husband. In California, I was always Jaime with a "J". Here, I was a mix of "J" and the Spanish "H". Betsy always used the "J"version. I was never bothered by whichever was used. With Billy, I seemed to be the gringo version at home and the Hispanic version in town.

Betsy said, "Jaime, I hope you'll stay again tonight, and if you want, I'll lead a simple service in the chapel tomorrow morning."

I thought I owed her a confession by now. "Would you believe me if I said your chapel is the only church I've ever been in? I never quite got my nerve up to join the Cardonas at the Catholic Church."

I was relieved by her response. "Well, there was a time I would have judged you harshly for that, but I also know the kind of childhood you've had. More importantly, my judging days are over, I hope and pray."

I said, "Then I accept your invitation."

With that, she was off to the south porch until it was time to think about dinner, as Billy and I rocked away not saying much of anything. Billy did say that since moving to the ranch neither his mom nor dad had been to church in town. He said his dad still sent the Methodists a check every month, and that he never was an every-Sunday member. Still, he was surprised they didn't seem to fret a bit about what the town might be saying about their lapsed ways.

I asked Billy, "Did you go to church when you lived up by Van Horn?"

He answered, "The only church I went to was 'saddlebag-baptist.' I'd go riding on the ranch on Sunday mornings so long as the mega-rich didn't need me attending to them for something in particular and the wind was less than forty miles an hour. It didn't matter to me if it was hot, cold or in between."

I got my nerve up to ask something that had always been on my mind. "You ever going to tell me why you left when you were sixteen? I'm not trying to pry."

He said, "I think you already know that the woman who resides here now bears no resemblance to the woman I knew all those years ago. Once she got 'saved,' she became a zealot and was determined I was going to be 'born again' come hell or high water. Up until her 'conversion' we were a pretty normal laid-back family as you would imagine with the dad we have.

"All that changed, and being the oldest, I will always contend I got the worst of it. Soon after I turned sixteen, she really mounted the pressure on me, and one day I'd had it. I thought if I said this, she'd leave me alone. I got right back in her face and I hollered, '*Fuck off!*' I couldn't believe myself that I'd said it. That was *not* a phrase we *ever* used in the Schlatter household! Well, she hollered back, '*Get out of my house!* I'll have no son *ever* use such language in front of me! The devil has your soul, and I'll not let *you* take your brother and sister with you over to *him!*'

"So, that is how I left that day and never went back."

I just said, "I get it now." Adding a little levity to my having taken him back to that day, I said, "I'm not surprised that word was not used in the Schlatter house. Obviously, you learned that one at school. Ernesto's kids don't need to rely on the school. He knows the word well—both in English and Spanish. He also knows he'd better never use it within earshot of Rosalinda."

Billy chuckled and said, "Badass Ernesto!"

All four of us were in the chapel that next morning. It would best be described as simplicity. Betsy had a couple Psalms she read and a well-chosen excerpt on "organized religion" from the Norris book that I had given her. She'd asked Billy to bring his harmonica to play *Amazing Grace*. She asked that we sit quietly for a few minutes and then if anyone wanted to say anything to feel free to do so.

I was surprised when Bill broke the silence saying simply, "I am so grateful for this place and for the healing that has been brought to our family."

A couple minutes passed when Billy said, "I am so grateful to be home and for Jaime's friendship—the first *real* friend I've ever had."

I felt like now I *should* say something but wasn't at all sure I could get it out without my voice breaking badly. When I thought I might be able to eke something out, I haltingly said, "I am overwhelmed with gratitude."

Betsy began singing a song I didn't know but clearly the other two did as they were quick to join her.

Blest be the tie that binds
our hearts in Christian love;
the fellowship of kindred minds
is like to that above.

Before our Maker's throne
we pour our ardent prayers;
our fears, our hopes, our aims are one,
our comforts and our cares.

We share each other's woes,
each other's burdens bear,
and often for each other flows
the sympathizing tear.

Then they repeated the first verse, and I joined in as best I could.

Blest be the tie that binds
our hearts in Christian love;
the fellowship of kindred minds
is like to that above.

As I listened closely to those words—digesting the beauty of them—I marveled at what I knew of so much Christian division which had, in fact, divided *this* house for *so long*. How could it be, when the message at its very core is this kind of peace and love? Why is it ever betrayed?

Chapter Thirty-one

Sunday after lunch, the phone rang. Billy answered it and said it was for me. I thought it must be Ernesto wanting to track me down about something. Instead it was Lupe.

"I understand you know Emma is ill. Her brother Claude called here saying that Emma wanted you to know she's going to a hospice in Midland. He said, 'She's not feeling well enough to drive and doesn't want me driving that far. She wants me to see if Jaime could drive us up there—today if at all possible.'"

"Good grief!" I exclaimed. "She was just diagnosed. Call him back and let him know I'm on my way. Then let Ernesto know I might miss work tomorrow. I may stay up there tonight. I'll just have to wait and see what's going on."

With that, I said my goodbyes and headed back to town. I had my little overnight bag from staying at the ranch, and so I didn't even run by the casita. Emma, not Claude, met me at the door. She whispered, "He's a basket case; that's why I needed you."

As she motioned me into the house she said, "I'm done for. They can't do anything for me and there is no way I can cope here. It may seem a little premature to move to hospice, but they say I will go downhill quick. It will just be better if I'm where Claude doesn't feel useless when he knows he is."

I said, "You're amazing."

"I'm not afraid to die, if that's what you mean," she said.

"I didn't want to say it quite that directly, but that is what I meant," I replied.

She said, "Claude feels cheated because he was supposed to die first. Now he doesn't know what he'll do. I think he needs to find an assisted-living place. You might help me work that into his mind as the best option. He can't stay out here on his own at his age."

Then she hollered, "Brother, Jaime is here. Are you ready?"

He came puttering down the hall from the back carrying two small suitcases—one for her and his own. I took them from him, and we went to their car. I just assumed they wouldn't want to crawl up into my truck and would instruct me otherwise if they didn't want me driving the car. They didn't.

As we started out of town I said, "I guess you know where we're going?"

Emma said, "Yes, I have the directions here. When we get past Odessa we'll have to start looking out for the exit."

Claude didn't say anything the whole trip. He sat in the back, Emma in the front seat. Emma was mostly her usual chipper self. In fact, she'd heard about Billy's flirtation at the Slo Poke Cafe, which amused her greatly. She wanted to know if he was serious. I said, "Who knows? It is hard to read exactly what goes on in that mind. I do know he considers me to be the first real friend he's ever had, and I think that's all there is to it. He has even said exactly that in front of his mom and dad. On that score, I would say the same is true for me. I've never had a close friend my own age, and I feel like he is someone I can confide in. I hope it is the same for him."

Emma said, "The food pantry has certainly had a windfall since Betsy left that church of hers. She and Bill are by far the biggest benefactor these days. She always includes a note whenever she sends their check to thank me for all I do for the community."

I said, "To hear Billy's take, the body snatchers took his mother for a time, and he's glad to have the mother back he knew as a small boy."

As we came down the last mountain towards the vast, flat, desolate country that makes up Reeves County, she sighed heavily and said, "I guess that was the last time I'll see those mountains. There will be many 'last time' things from here on."

With that she remained silent until it was time to help me navigate the last few miles towards our destination.

Someone from the hospice saw us drive up and was out the door with a wheelchair. Instead of taking the chair to Emma as she got out of the car, the girl rolled the chair over to Claude who was getting out on the driver's side. Emma looked to see what her brother would do. He just sat down in the chair and was wheeled in.

We both chuckled as she said to me, "You see what I mean? In his mind, I'm supposed to be taking care of him. What a caregiver he would be!"

The head day-nurse met us inside and had a peculiar look on his face. He asked rather haltingly, "Are you Ms. Meijer?"

She laughed and said, "Yes, that's just my older brother, who is used to being waited on."

He replied, "I'll get you right to your room. Do you *want* a wheelchair?"

She said, "I'm fine to walk, and this is our good friend, Jaime Cruz. He will also be my emergency contact in addition to my dear brother."

The nurse, who had talked to Emma on the phone about her check-in, introduced himself. "I'm Luke Edwards. Nice to meet you, Jaime."

I realized in that moment that technology was going to tighten its grip on me. I was going to *have* to get a phone, and it might just as well be a cell phone.

This was my first experience with hospice and so far it was an encouraging one. They seemed to care little about a formal check-in, there was no sitting in a waiting room as you have to do in every hospital and doctor's office, the place looked much more like a comfortable home even with its necessary medical beds and gear around the room, and the staff all projected a friendly, compassionate demeanor.

They also had a room ready for Claude. Emma said to the woman who came to show him where it was, "You might need to remind him he's here to visit me and not moving in."

You could see she was quickly endearing herself to the staff, as was Claude in his own naturally oblivious state.

Claude was soon back, and we sat and visited until it was time for their dinner. I said I should be going and waited for her to cue me as to whether she expected me to be around the next day.

Emma said, "I will call Lupe every day that I can and will give them her number to get ahold of you. I don't expect you to miss work sitting here with me. We'll be fine."

I said, "I will get a phone and get that number to the office, and I will gladly visit as often or not as you see fit."

She responded, "Always call first. There's no point in driving two and a half hours to find out I'm out of it or dead. As long as I'm coherent I'd enjoy the visits, though if they up my morphine—

which they will soon—I may doze off in the middle of the conversation."

I felt like a dunce then. I said to Claude, "I'm here in your car. What are you going to do?"

Claude said, "I'm not going anywhere in the next few days. Don't worry about it. Besides, I know my sister wants me here to convince me to go into assisted living somewhere."

I left, saying, "I'll be back Tuesday unless for some reason Ernesto can't live without me."

Chapter Thirty-two

I would be running the roads for the next two weeks. I was certainly glad I bought the F-150 when I did as I didn't think it wise to drive someone else's car without them going along. A couple times, Billy wanted to know if I wanted him to ride along saying he'd wait in the lobby if Emma wanted me all to herself. I was glad to have another driver and the company along the way and quickly accepted his offer.

Emma was glad to have Billy in the room. Whenever a different staff member would come in she'd say, "How many dying women have two handsome men to visit them so often?"

"Not many," they would say.

On one of my visits with Billy, she said to me, "I told people for years that I was an atheist, but I've never forgotten what you said to me about your view to that when you left California. Do you remember what you said?"

I said, "Not specifically, but I could about guess."

She said, "You told me you couldn't be an atheist because you lacked the certainty that would require. At best, you said, you were nothing in particular."

"That was pretty accurate," I said. "I just didn't remember actually saying it out loud to someone else," to which Billy gave a quiet chuckle from the corner of the room where he was seated.

She said, "I've been nothing in particular ever since. That's the influence you've had on me! I've even talked my even firmer, former-atheist brother into being nothing in particular."

I asked, "Will I be a disappointment to you if I have become something in particular?"

"That would depend," she said. "What in particular is it you think you have become?"

I said, "I think I'm a full-fledged member of the church of mercy over judgment."

She was beginning to fade. Her eyes closed. Softly she smiled just a bit and whispered, "Sign me up."

The next morning I got a call on my cell phone before leaving for work. It was Luke. "Ms. Meijer passed away peacefully about

5:00 this morning. She never regained consciousness after you left. Whatever she might have said to you were her last words."

My first question was, "How is Claude?"

"Coping," was all he said.

"Should I come get him? I know you and Emma already made her arrangements. I'm not quite sure what to do about Claude."

Luke said, "The good news is we had someone from a nearby assisted-living center come pick him up a couple days ago. Emma wasn't really coherent enough to know we'd done this. He is going to move in there and said he hopes you can help get their things sold in Fort Davis."

"Of course, I will do that," I said.

Luke continued, "Emma asked that we not have a memorial service of any kind. Do you think that will be understood back home?"

I said, "Emma and I would be of one mind in that regard. If they don't like it, tough shit."

Then he said, "Her instructions were that she was to be cremated right away—no embalming. Were you aware of that?"

"Yes, wholly aware. And that I am to scatter her ashes in a particular spot here in the mountains."

He said, "Very good. I will proceed with that, assuming Claude signs off on what is needed on this end."

Next, I called Rosalinda. Not only had she known Emma from the pantry, she had assumed her duties for the time being. I said to Rosalinda, "Emma had one request for the future of the pantry."

"What's that?" she asked.

"That it *never* be called the Emma Meijer Memorial Food Pantry —not unless you want her ghost haunting the place."

Chapter Thirty-three

Claude was soon settled into his new home and quite happy with it. Sara would miss his predictability at the Slo Poke Cafe. It took me a few months to wrap things up with Emma and Claude's home in Fort Davis, and to my surprise Claude never did want to come back. He gave me a list of what he wanted brought to him and that was that. I even sold his car to someone in Alpine. His driving days were done. He gave me a generous stipend for my work, which I donated to the food pantry though I never told him.

Since that first Sunday together in the chapel, I had become a regular fixture—staying Friday and Saturday nights at the ranch and attending "church" on Sundays. I really was concerned about wearing out my welcome. I even thought maybe Jean and Mary-Alice would wonder what was going on with my constant presence since every time they were there so was I. If it did bother them, they hid it well. They, like Bill, Betsy and Billy made me feel like I was supposed to be there. The girls had started joining us in the chapel on Sundays at least once a month.

In fact, the only one who seemed to be a bit of a misfit, and who they were always glad to see leave for some other short visit down the road, was Brett and whatever clump of family was in tow with him. There was never any invitation offered for the grandchildren camping out with Grandma and Grandpa in the big house or any suggestion that Billy and I yield "our" rooms and stay in the bunkhouse.

During the week, I lived my life with the Cardonas. The weekends my life was with the Schlatters. It was, in so many respects, an abundance of riches.

Ernesto, Roberto and I had all the work we needed and a little more than any of us wanted from time to time—especially when it was time to crank out a few thousand adobes. I had designs for two other houses in the queue for whenever we could get to them. So far, both clients were waiting for Ernesto rather than taking the plans to another builder. Our deal was, if we built it, the plans were free. If they wanted to "own" the plans, we'd charge hourly based on how much they were revised.

I didn't see house drawing as a "vocation" any more than I did packing tomatoes or writing songs. Billy and I did spend our Friday nights making music and had soon set half a dozen of Bill's lyrics and poems to music. Billy even got a local cowboy performer in Alpine to add a couple of them to his repertoire. Much to Betsy's chagrin, one was "Wall Street *Bandidos*"—*Lyrics by Bill J. Schlatter, Sr., Music by Jaime E. Cruz.*

She said to Billy, "Couldn't you tell him Lyrics by Anonymous."

He said, "As Jaime would say, 'giving credit where credit is due.'"

The truth is, the song was a hit with any crowd. We both gave the performer permission to put it on his next CD. It remained to be seen if that would come to fruition. He doesn't move too fast on releasing new albums since they always include all new material. It takes a while to accumulate a collection's worth.

Billy said, "If "*Bandidos*" ever becomes a top-ten hit, you two are gonna wish you'd gotten a royalty agreement in writing."

Bill said, "I don't think for now that'll keep me up at night."

As another Christmas approached, Jean and Mary-Alice asked Betsy if she would mind if a group of people from their church in Marfa came out to the ranch on the first Saturday in December for an Advent Quiet Day. While part of the day would be spent in the chapel, people would need to be free to come in the house for meals and to sit quietly and read. There would be no group discussion. They discussed some approaches for the time in the chapel and Betsy, with one of her epiphanies suggested, "To guide the reflections for the day, why don't we have fifteen-minute-or-so services scattered across the day—say 7:30, 10:00, noon and 2:30? The last one would end in the dismissal for the day since that seems like the timeframe you are talking about. We could have a simple reading at each according to whatever theme is to be reflected upon for the day. If there is to be any music, it will just be chanting or a cappella. We could include that chanted version from the monastery out east that we use for the Lord's Prayer at one of the four services. Is this anything you think the group might like?"

Jean said, "I think it is certainly worth pitching to the priest."

Mary-Alice said, "I don't think he even plans to attend. He'll be relieved he doesn't have to do anything to make it happen."

They both liked their priest, but to quote Jean, "He likes the collar more than he likes actual work—especially if it alters his rather flexible and comfortable schedule."

Betsy said, "Your father will probably find something to do on the ranch rather than attend. Do we need to run Billy and Jaime off as well or is this coed?"

Jean said, "Men are invited."

Betsy said, "Sounds interesting. Go ahead."

The Saturday before the "Quiet Day," I had a chance to sit down with Betsy and talk to her about my Bible story encounter with Joseph and his coat of many colors. I had long wanted to talk to her about it to see if this disconnection between the story and the Bible was a one-off or more the norm than not. Since that first story had bothered me so much, it took a while before I dipped my toe in a second time, but again, I encountered the same disconnected result.

"Betsy," I said, "don't take this as some way of trying to trip you up. Quite some time ago, Lupe gave me a CD of Bible stories and a Bible. The first one I listened to was about Joseph—the Joseph sold into slavery by his brothers. I assume you learned that as a Bible story, is that right?"

"Yes," she said.

"Tell me how you were taught the story," I said.

She recited it just as it had been told on the CD.

I then asked, "And is that how you believe the story to be and would tell others now?"

"I'm not sure what you mean," she said rather puzzled.

Without getting a Bible and reading verse by verse, I laid out for her all the different aspects of the story, why they bothered me, and that how the normal telling of the story seemed to contradict or, at best, ignore very important parts of the account. I'd been over it so many times, there were verses I could quote word for word.

She looked almost dumbfounded. Then she said, "Is it possible the Catholic Bible is that much different from the ones the Protestants use? I don't think all that is in there."

I said I didn't know if I had a Catholic Bible or not. She went and retrieved the version her old church uses and the one the Methodists use. I remembered the important chapters and she flipped right to them. She read quietly for several minutes.

"Jaime," she said, "you *clearly* have the gift of not being burdened down by taking what is fed you as what you have to believe. I would say your rendition of the account is far more accurate than the story we teach—which is pretty sad. Not sad that you have given this such a level of thought—sad that the rest of us, who think we know all about the Bible, have not."

Billy was sitting there with us and hadn't said a word. I almost forgot he was there since I was sitting facing Betsy.

Billy said, "I admit to willful ignorance when it comes to the Bible, but what little I know leaves me confounded as to moral judgments made when all the characters in the Old Testament had the most dysfunctional families possible—starting with murder in the 'first family' and all manner of complications after that. Then Jesus came along and seemed to say, 'This world is all right—you can make it better—just like heaven if you want.' What did we do with that? Start preachin' *heaven, heaven, heaven, hell, hell, hell!* It's all we ever heard—not 'Thy kingdom come. Thy will be done. *On earth!*'"

Betsy reflected, "In your own ways, you two boys have both hit the nail on the head as to how I lost my way for so many years. I checked my mind at the door. No more! I'll never hear a Bible story again without going back and digging into it for myself."

Chapter Thirty-four

Betsy liked the Advent Quiet Day so much she asked Bill if he was okay with her extending the invitation to do it the first Saturday of each month. Still delighted by her departure from the fundamentalist crowd, he gave an enthusiastic "yes" to her request. He added, "The beauty of this place is hardly ours to selfishly hoard —it should be shared."

Betsy asked Jean to see if she thought any would be interested. She got a very enthusiastic "yes" back from the Marfa bunch as well. The Marfa group also loved the format of the services in the chapel and wanted to make those permanent fixtures. And so it was on the first Saturday of January and each month thereafter, all agreed—whether a holiday or not—the first Saturday was now Quiet Day at the ranch.

Billy said to his mom, "As long as your expanding plans don't interfere with our Friday family music night, we're good with it."

I assumed he and I were the "we." I'm rarely certain when he uses the plural pronoun exactly who he has included.

Rosalinda's routine had changed some as well. She was officially the new director of the food pantry. Ernesto did everything possible to avoid our crew working on Saturdays and would help her out on distribution day. Billy and I were also regulars, and the four of us had our long-standing, post-pantry lunch at the Slo Poke Cafe following each distribution.

Bill and Betsy had just closed on the sale of their house in town when Billy spotted a black Jag at the Slo Poke Cafe.

He said, "I bet the gay guys from Dallas are here."

"We don't know they're gay," I said.

"Right," was his response. We were no sooner inside than the forthright Billy went up to two men in a booth. "Hi, I'm Billy Schlatter. I believe you just bought my childhood home."

"Hi, Billy, I'm John and this is James."

I was standing back from the exchange, but Billy grabbed my arm and tugged me towards him. "This is my sometime live-in, Jaime."

I shook my head and said, "The boy exaggerates."

Billy borrowed my line, "Of a kind."

They were left wondering what we were all about.

Settled in the booth with Ernesto and Rosalinda, Billy said, "Those guys over there are the gay guys who bought Mom and Dad's house."

I reiterated, "We don't know they are gay."

Rosalinda said, "You two look far more gay than they do."

"Oh, thank you so much, Rosalinda," I said.

"In this place, you know it's true," Ernesto chuckled.

Loyal, dependable Sara had grown accustomed to our antics, and Billy amused her greatly. Ernesto and Rosalinda were also entertained by how playful Billy loved to be in public. I was a good sport about it—even knowing half the town now probably assumed we were gay lovers. He would have his arm around my shoulder as we'd come into the restaurant and do the same as we left. If he thought someone was looking on with some degree of disgust, it egged him on all the more—he would hold my hand or more likely, slap me on the hind end as we left.

After a pat on the backside happened a third time, I finally had the nerve to say to him outside the Slo Poke Cafe, "You've got the great ass. I should be spanking yours."

Typical Billy response—"Oh, I'm flattered you've noticed!"

"You're a mess," I said.

"But I'm your mess," he said.

"Of a kind."

He just put his arm around my shoulder again as we walked across the parking lot towards his truck. It wasn't like he tried to be some straight-laced, role-model son when we were around his folks. He made no secret of his desire to spend virtually all his free time with me and was just as likely to walk with his arm around me at home. Word even got back to his mother that he'd slapped my butt in the restaurant and when she heard it, she just laughed. She told Bill about it at our Friday night dinner.

Bill just shook his head and said, "As long as you don't compete with Ernesto on New Year's Eve on drag outfits."

Betsy said, "Don't give him any ideas!"

140

Billy had the grace to say, "Mother, you needn't worry about that. I see someone from your old church just about every time we're in the Slo Poke Cafe, and I just can't help letting them see life can be fun."

Then Billy added, "Now, I can't speak for Jaime. Could be he'll come as Judy Garland one of these holidays."

I just said, "Could be not!"

Bill reassured his wife, "Honey, you don't need to worry about me going drag either. Now, I can't guarantee your daughter might not show up sometime as James Dean."

Betsy chuckled and said, "Well, that might be all right. She dresses like him most of the time anyway."

Billy caught that. "Gender discrimination," he said.

I offered, "I'll get you a kilt so long as you promise only to wear it when Jean comes over. "

Betsy's mind was expanding on the picture of that. "Well, now a kilt might be okay if you take up the bagpipes."

Bill set his condition to such an undertaking, "He'll need to practice bagpipes down at the bunkhouse!"

Billy said, "Oh, I forgot to tell you, Jaime and I met John and James who bought the old house. They were at the Slo Poke Cafe — still driving the black Jag."

Betsy replied, "We never did meet them. Annie seemed to like them a lot, and your father is now their banker — carrying their mortgage."

I said, "They look good for it. I doubt they will have to be evicted for defaulting on their loan."

Billy laughed, "I introduced Jaime as my sometimes live-in."

Bill shook his head, "Good lord. You're lucky Jaime puts up with you."

I was thoroughly enjoying my weekends at the ranch. Friday night was always a time of music, laughing, sometimes serious conversation, sometimes just sitting by the fire on a cold night or rocking out on the porch so long as we wouldn't freeze or be blown out of our chairs.

Saturdays were split between the food pantry and the Slo Poke Cafe, Quiet Day, and one or two free Saturdays when Billy would usually persuade me to go over to Sallie's, saddle up the horses and ride around the ranches. As private as she seemed to me, Sallie would from time to time ride with us. She never had much to say but seemed to like the company. I could see how much she liked Billy. Who wouldn't?

Our Sundays in the chapel had become a consistent routine— Jean and Mary-Alice joining us with more and more frequency. I was shocked when even Sallie started showing up—not every Sunday but more often than not.

I learned some simple hymns I could play on my guitar, and I discovered that the mandolin was actually Bill's, and he was quite good. Betsy was the master planner on who was providing the music for any given Sunday. She always led the service and usually included some scripture and a reading from some other book. Some Sundays it was all poetry—even some of Bill's, though "Wall Street *Bandidos*" never made the cut.

Billy and I had practiced chanting some of the Psalms. We practiced only when his mother wasn't around so as to not get snagged in before we thought our effort was up to muster. Once we auditioned a few we thought were good enough, she made us a regular addition each Sunday. We sang the monk's version of the Lord's Prayer every week. The service was a modest, humble affair and never lasted more than thirty to forty minutes. Betsy would spend another fifteen minutes or so in silence afterwards. Sometimes one or more of us would stay as well—usually not.

When the girls were there on Sundays, they always spent Saturday night in the bunkhouse and came up to the house for dinner. Bill loved to hear about their take on all things Marfa. The most common theme was the revolving door of "city folk" who showed up so enchanted by its "remote charm" and then concluded there was "nothing to do" there. Mary-Alice was always glad to "name names" in this regard.

One evening, Mary-Alice went on a bit of a tear about it. She said, "There is a trend now that I fear is only going to get worse. I don't have to tell you it wasn't but a few years ago we didn't have to rollup the sidewalks at night because the town was so dead they were never unrolled in the morning. Money has now come into town, and a few bringing it in seem to be there for keeps. It's the transients we worry about. They buy some ramshackle on the cheap, double that to fix it up and then, when they are bored, they try to take what they've got in it and sell it for four times that."

I still had never even bothered driving to Marfa so I had no image of any of the "before and after." I said, "Surely it's not *quite* that bad."

Jean jumped in and said, "Oh, it's that bad, and Mary-Alice is right. It is only trending towards more extreme cases as these people with more money than sense 'market' their 'charming adobe for sale in the Santa Fe of West Texas.'"

Mary-Alice said, "Marfa is like Santa Fe about as much as an old Ford Pinto is like a new Lincoln Town Car."

Billy interjected, "My own preference would be a black Jaguar over a Town Car."

Bill said, "It wouldn't ever be black out here running these ranch roads. You might want to get one of those colors where you can't tell if it's dirty or not."

To which Billy responded, "I don't know. I overhead a lady in Van Horn say her next car was gonna be red because nobody sees those dirt-colored cars, and someone was always pullin' out in front of her or backin' into her."

Bill stated flatly, "You can get me one of those convertibles they make so I can ride around in the cool night air and gawk at the stars. I guess the horsepower would be wasted on me idling down these roads."

Jean said, "You two sure know how to focus."

Then she added, "You can already see how much this is straining the poorer people in town when the houses they could afford to rent or buy are being snatched up as second, third or fourth "homes" for their rich buyers. All the young people can do is leave. Take us even, who make a damn reasonable living and bought that nice house just two blocks from the courthouse square and paid what was a very fair price. We're not far from where if we had to buy the same house today, we couldn't afford it—not even close if it keeps goin' the way it's goin'."

Mary-Alice jumped back in, "The city and county aren't complaining that we can tell because they see assessments going up and so their income is going up. And there *are* businesses opening up catering to the out-of-towners making for a few piss-poor-paying service jobs, but not a local economy that gives either one of us much confidence in any sustainability."

Jean said, "One big pop of the bubble in this country and all the air is going to go out of the Santa Fe of West Texas."

Mary-Alice said, "We could be wrong, of course. We have the humility to acknowledge that. Still, we can't divorce ourselves from the present reality that this boom cycle is good for a very small number of people—like it isn't hard enough already out here to keep the next generation from leaving."

Bill said, "As you've given some credit where credit is due already, I'll offer just a bit more. Those you say have come with money—not as transients but putting down roots even if they still spend considerable time flying around the country or the world because they can—have helped bring that town back to life. Ten years ago, I'd have said Alpine and Fort Davis were gonna make it come what may. I thought Marfa was dead and was just waiting for the few old families there to die out."

Billy looked at me, "I need to take you to Marfa and 'show you the town.' I haven't been there myself since I was in school. Sounds like we need to check it out."

Jean offered, "Come spend a night or two. We'll show you all the hot spots including the big gay bar."

Mary-Alice laughed, "Yeah, that would be the four bar stools we have out on our back patio."

Betsy exclaimed, "Here I've been to a gay bar and didn't even know it!"

Bill said, "She'll be wanting to figure out how to get that news to her old church group next."

Monday through Friday, Billy was rancher and maintenance man, and I was mason tender, sometimes carpenter, house designer and tractor driver.

I was still waiting for my Cardona invitation to their New Year's Eve party—I'd yet to see Ernesto in his customary roles. Maybe my missing the annual Cardona Easter gathering at Chuy and Lupe's recently now voided any consideration I might have to attend any more Cardona family affairs. Billy started dropping hints at the Slo Poke Cafe hoping he could wangle both of us an invitation.

After the third time of hinting with no success, I said, "I know we'd both like to go, but I think we need to leave it be. They know we want to come—I'm not sure what's going on. They might know someone there who would have a problem with us for some reason —maybe one of their relatives attends your mom's old church. Maybe it is just genuinely family only, though that's not very characteristic from my own experiences with them."

He said, "I guess you are right. I'll leave it alone. It will happen or not."

Then we both had a realization at the same time and almost said in unison, "When have we ever invited them to anything?"

Chapter Thirty-five

Billy and I began to think about our realization regarding our own lack of social interaction with the wider Cardona clan. This only led us to another topic altogether—the gringo-Hispanic divide that always runs as an undercurrent at best and in more blatant forms in some communities. In California, it was my experience that using the word gringo would bring about glares of contempt as there were those who considered the term racist. Out here, you'd have been pretentious not to allow yourself to be called a gringo. The term was as much a self-identifier inside the white community as it was between the white and brown communities. It never bothered anyone who I ever knew and certainly never bothered me. I was on that line where I was called "gringo" one time and "Mexican" the next—most often by the same person—Ernesto. He liked to change it up according to however it fit his jovial mood at the moment.

I set out the question to Billy. "When I moved here, semi-bilingual as I am and with the name *Jaime* Cruz, I was taken in without any suspicion or reservation. I see how the little old ladies at the food pantry hug on you and smile just because you look like your grandpa—well, that and they always like hugging a handsome man—hell they even hug me sometimes. But I digress.

"I'm not sure you stuck around here long enough as a kid to know the answer to this. Did your family live under an inherent and very distinct segregation, and isn't that still the reality? That is to say, it seems to be the whites who mostly own the ranches and the browns who are their help."

Billy knew I was serious, but he still had his own way of facing things. He answered asking, "So are you really saying our friendship stands in the way of you getting invited to New Year's Eve at Ernesto's, and if you'd quit coming to the ranch, you'd soon be included?"

"I'm not saying for sure that's the case with them, but if it were, I'm saying I would not willing to give up my friendship with you or your mom and dad. But not to put too fine a point on it, yes, I fear that could be true—even as we remain close to Ernesto and

Rosalinda and how they are entertained by you at the Slo Poke Cafe twice a month."

"That's a hell of a way to look at it," he said. "I'm the free entertainment."

"Well, you are worth every penny," I assured him.

"Two pennies times zero," he said.

We both smiled.

Digging into his family a bit he said, "My mother, for the longest time treated 'the help' like shit. She was better if Dad was around but if not, all you can do is to describe it as master-slave, I'm sorry to say. It only went from bad to worse after she was 'born again' and started hearing sermons about God's 'divine order' for 'mankind.'"

I admitted, "I got my own version of that when I first heard about your mom from Lupe who knew the woman who worked for her when they still lived in town."

Billy said, "I can imagine. I have seen enough intermarrying between the two communities to see how often they sorta have to 'choose' between one or the other of the families. We divide by color, by church, by economic status and even by weight, height and quality of teeth."

I said, "Even that's but a partial list and each one's too true."

He said, "I don't suppose our friendship can be much of a bridge since you have no roots here and mine come from the 'ownership class.'"

I asserted, "Your dad's integrity and your mom's—now that she realizes her integrity is not defined by blindly following some preacher's idea of right and wrong—are evident enough to everyone in town I've ever heard talk of them. Chuy says your dad is 'the salt of the earth.'"

"That he is," Billy said.

I said, "As for the generation before that, I've never heard anyone say much of anything, but that may only be due to me not knowing any of the older generation. Lupe's mom, Elma, is about the only one I've ever been around, and it's not like we talk about the old social order of Fort Davis.

"The other reality is that even as a Cruz, perhaps because I told Chuy and Lupe what I did about my unreligious background, I've never been invited to Mass and have no comfort level with wandering through the door to check it out. Isn't that strange? I'd feel even more awkward in many a protestant church. What do they believe? At least I had some spiritual formation from Merton on the Catholic faith—even if most of his writings on it were essentially a foreign language to me."

"You like *La Capilla de la Rosa* at the ranch, don't you?" he asked.

"That's a good name for it. Where did you come up with that?" I asked.

"It literally just hit me," he said,

I got back to the subject. "To me, our chapel times are the epitome of the old Latin saying I once shared with Chuy: 'Where true love and charity are, God is there.' I told Chuy that Lupe quilted that love into every quilt just as every moment we spend together in the chapel affirms the same for me. God is there. Love is there.

"The first prayer I ever prayed was in the Cardona casita. It was my first night in town. At the time I thought, 'I don't know if I'm praying to God or to the cosmos or if there is a difference.' I would change that a little now—only to say I do know I pray to love."

Billy smiled and asked, "Did we mean to get this deep?"

"It is pretty deep for our simple minds," I said.

We sat quietly reflecting a moment when Billy added, "If you and I have a 'spiritual practice,' it is that we aren't going to let other people's toxicity, even if it is well-disguised, dominate our lives. I'll even go one step further and say *our life*—as I feel, for reasons I don't myself comprehend, you and I are joined in one life. Am I crazy?"

All I could say to that was, "If you are, I am as well. I feel *exactly* the same."

Chapter Thirty-six

When I arrived at the ranch the following Friday night, Billy informed me that we were going riding the next day. We had never planned that in advance other weekends when we did go riding, but I didn't really think anything about it. He was his usual jovial self Friday night, and our time with his mom and dad as delightful as always. Well, almost. Brett was there with his wife—same one— which was slowly nearing a new record in longevity though that wasn't saying much. They, of course, were staying in the bunkhouse, and Bill somehow managed to "turn them out to pasture" almost as soon as we were done eating.

It may be this latest wife would stick. They were not bad people. Just dull as dust. Brett still had not awakened to the natural world around him—one he was reared in the midst of. Instead, he was all about image and cars and gated communities. Fortunately, he made enough to support his habits including the complicated child-support arrangements mandated by the courts.

And it must be said, hope did spring eternal from the reunited family for a great awakening in Brett's life.

After they left that evening, Bill said, "Two down and one to go. This last one is the only thick-headed one in the bunch. Must be middle-child syndrome. Whatever it is, I wish he would shut up once in a while."

Betsy mildly shook her head in disapproval of her husband's blunt comments, probably only because he seemed to be saying them to me more than anyone else in particular.

Betsy announced she was going to go to the chapel for a bit—no doubt to pray for son number two—which prompted Billy to remember his revelation during our recent conversation. "Mom, we gave the chapel a name, *La Capilla de la Rosa*."

"I rather like that," she said. "I might even have to get a little plaque."

We three men went out to the rockers on the ridge-side porch staring off into the vast expanse with just the faintest light still off where the sun, now gone, continued on its course towards beginning the day for the living world in other lands.

After breakfast the next morning, Billy and I were off to Sallie's to saddle up the horses. Billy had said that if Sallie wanted to ride with us, he was going to find some work excuse as to dissuade her. Clearly, he had something on his mind he wanted to tackle away from everyone else. What that might be remained a complete mystery to me. I didn't think it was some "chapter two" of our conversation of social and religious issues. When he was ready, he would tell me.

We trotted along for thirty minutes or so—I never do wear a watch—and we stopped at a rather spectacular outcropping of rock.

I said, "I'm surprised we haven't ridden here before."

He explained, "I was here as a kid a few times with Dad and had forgotten all about it. He and I rode out here on Wednesday. That's what I want to talk to you about."

If anything, it was getting more mysterious rather than less. We tied the horses to a piñon pine and he climbed up—me following—onto the rock and sat down.

Several minutes passed before he finally spoke. "Dad wanted to talk to me about my 'intentions,' was the word he used, as pertains to you."

Even with all of Billy's shenanigans, this was the very first time I felt any sense of nervousness and dread from anything he might say.

He started out, "Perhaps you could tell last night from what he said to you after Brett left. Of a kind, he sees you as more of a son to him than his own son. And I don't mean by some sentimental trifle. I mean to him you are part of this family. He gets that we are best friends. I think he trusts the fact that for us it has not been something sexual like so many of Brett's exploits—though he made it clear that just as with Jean, if that is who we are, then he has no problem with it. You and I both know that already, I believe, but he felt the need to say it."

Then he stopped to ask, chuckling a bit as he asked it, "Am I making you as uncomfortable now as he made me?"

I said, "Possibly."

He continued, "Maybe this will put you a little bit at ease. He can't imagine how, if I ever marry, you and I could maintain the kind of friendship and camaraderie that we have now. At the same time he has the same concern for me if you were to marry—which he thinks a more likely scenario just given the fact that you are in town a lot and may meet someone while, as you and he know, I'm a ranch dude perfectly content to stay out here with minimal runnin' to town. And I'm certainly not looking for a wife."

I interrupted to say, "I would ask why that is, but since I relate to it completely, I feel I know the answer even though I couldn't articulate it well if I had to."

He continued, "That makes two of us."

He grinned widely and snickered. Then he said, "Dad asked me, 'Can two middle-aged men make a life together when they are friends and not sharing a bed in the long haul, or is one of you going to move on to greener pastures?' In one of my wiser moments I said that would take both of us to answer that question, which I then followed up with saying, 'And my smart-ass self might say, what makes you think we might not still get cold on some winter night and crawl into bed together to keep warm?' He just smiled and said, 'I've already said I don't care.'

"So before I go on to part two of the conversation with Dad, I'm asking you the same question about intentions. Can you and I make a life together when we are friends and not sharing a bed in the long haul, or are you going to move on to greener pastures? I'll answer for myself—I'm in for the long haul and hope you are too."

I said, "Well, if I were a hugger and kisser I'd do both right now. I still can't really sort out my future and how I fit exactly, but as I said when we last talked, I'm not willing to give up my friendship with you or your mom and dad."

Billy stood up and said, "*Stand* up!"

"What are you doing?" I asked while following his orders.

He didn't kiss me nor did I kiss him, but I did get that hug I had longed for all those many months ago. I was sure he was crying. I know I was. We stood holding each other a long time.

Then he had to return to crazy Billy. Still holding me close he took my arms from around his back and lowered them until one hand was on each of his ass cheeks.

With my usual little chuckle that he so often inspired, I said, "You're a mess."

And he said, "But I'm your mess."

Chapter Thirty-seven

As Billy and I rode towards Sallie's to put the horses up and head back to the house, I said, "What was that part two of the conversation with your dad you were going to talk about. Is now the time?"

"As good a time as any," he said. "In fact, if we get back home and I haven't talked about it, I'll get my near middle-aged backside whooped for failing to do so.

"By the way, I asked Dad if he knew where you lived. Of course, he knew you lived in Chuy and Lupe's casita, but he wasn't at all sure where they lived. I drove him by, and he agreed that a Chihuahua would need to give advance warning if he wanted to turn around."

I interjected, "That metaphor amuses you, doesn't it?"

"As a matter of fact," he replied, "part two is that Dad and Mom really want to figure out a way for you to move out to the ranch. They love you spending the weekend with us, but as Dad says Mom says, 'Living here some and living there some isn't a good, long-term strategy for making a life together.'"

I wanted to say, "wise woman," but thought it better just to hear where this was going. I did repeat that last line out loud, "Making a life together."

Billy went on with what clearly was a work in progress as to how he could talk about all this. "Dad says from building the house he's pretty sure you already are clued in that the ranch didn't build the house. His oil rights did. By the way, what you may not know about that is how Dad wishes he didn't depend on that income. He is a most diligent steward of all he has, as you well know. He has always tried to use that money, in his words, 'to make something better while a lot of people only make things worse.'"

"Never was a truer word spoken," I said.

"Dad's point being, he could bring me back because of the oil money and not because of the ranch income. Probably nobody in town knows this, and Mom and Dad would never want it known, but the only reason Sallie can afford the help she has is because Dad pays for it and any other capital expenses she has. He has no ownership claim on the ranch and would never ask for one, but he's the reason these ranches not only survive but thrive."

To allow time for the conversation, we were barely moving on the horses. In fact, the horse I always ride, Chaco, kept stopping to nibble on some good grama. Then he'd set the slow pace for Billy's horse, Ole Blue, whose name was derived from the horse's eyes, as we made our way back to their pen.

Then Billy said, "Let me lay out what they want and you'll see the parts of the problem. People have generally assumed that since Sallie never married, the ranch would come back into our family. As I learned on Wednesday, it is a little more defined than that. For tax purposes and other legal requirements I don't fully have a handle on at this point, both ranches are in trusts with Dad and Sallie as trustees to both—Dad as primary. I had no idea this was the case. The trusts, now that I'm home, already have me as the head once Dad retires or 'goes up on that ridge' as he put it.

"Mom and Dad would like for Sallie to come live in our wing of the house and for you and me to move into her place—which is, of course, the original ranch house. Dad laughed and said, 'With that house Jaime drew it will be a big step down, but when Mother and I are gone you can always move over here if you want.' Then he laughed and said, 'I'm not moving your mother over to the old house. She'd only go kicking and screaming. It would *not* be pretty.'

"You've never been in Sallie's house but it's hardly a ramshackle. It's been kept up and modernized over the years. It has a kind of last-century look about it, but it's pretty nice.

"Anyway, the problem as they see it in the short run is twofold. One, they aren't sure how you'd feel about giving up your job in town to live out here full-time as they don't see how going to and from work everyday would be much fun. It would only make a long day's work that much longer. Two, Sallie has had that live-in helper for years. Mom and Dad can't see how or why we'd want her living with us and doubts very much the woman would live in the same house with two men even if we wanted to keep her on. Neither Mom nor Dad wants her living in your room back in our part of the house.

153

"The woman is getting pretty old. They really hope she tells Sallie sooner rather than later that she's ready to retire. According to Dad, Sallie already is making accommodations for her lack of being able to do what she used to do, to the point she's not really much help to Sallie anymore. Dad has always set aside a little retirement money for her in addition to Social Security. Dad told Sallie, 'Don't you think it's time to lay out for her what her income is going to look like if she retires? I'd even throw in a cash gift with it.' Sallie said, 'We gotta think about where she's gonna live if she doesn't have any idea of that herself.' Dad agreed that might be the biggest problem.

"The old woman does have plenty of relatives in town. Mom, Dad and Sallie just hope someone steps up to take her in at her age.

"Sallie is definitely winding down herself. She even said to me a couple weeks back, 'If you hadn't come home when you did, I was going to have to hire someone to keep this place going.'

"So you see, if Sallie winds down—she'll never quit altogether as long as she can get on the back of a horse—then as Mom, Dad and I see it, we really need you to help me out with what will be a fully rejoined ranch, run as one operation. Dad says he is much less resistant to retiring altogether than Sallie. He'd be content to sit on the south porch and look at the grass and cattle—maybe take to writing more poetry. Of course, he had to add, 'When I'm in my rocker on that porch, I'd better never see anything that shows the place going downhill.'"

"I don't think he has to worry about that given what the son has learned from the father," I said.

We paused our conversation long enough to put the horses up, say a few words to Sallie—who was shoeing her own horse—and jumped in the pickup and headed for the house.

Billy said, "So the big question Mom and Dad are going to want to know other than are you all in, is if you are going to quit that job, move out of that casita and start learning how to ranch. I'd say you've got about three more minutes to formulate your answer because I'm pretty sure they will be eagerly waiting for us when we get there."

Part IV

Chapter Thirty-eight

"Eagerly waiting" was the right choice of words. Both were out in the rockers with a view to the road awaiting our arrival. Both got up and walked towards the truck.

Betsy asked, "Did you have a nice ride, boys?"

"Great ride!" Billy answered for us.

Bill asked, "Come to any profound conclusions?"

"I'll have to let Jaime speak to that point," Billy said.

The allotted three minutes I was given—not even knowing quite how the question or questions might be put to me—hadn't yielded anything that I knew I was going to say. I just opened my mouth to see what came out.

"Billy had reached his conclusions before the conversation ever started," I said. "My conclusions are: I need to let Ernesto know he's going to have to hire some new help pretty soon; and I need to learn how to work on a ranch. I feel I've already got a pretty good idea of what life is going to be like with this crazy guy."

Betsy stepped quickly to me and hugged me, and Bill hugged the two of us, and of course that just made Billy hug the mess of us. Once untangled from our instinctive affection of the moment, Bill said, "We needn't make a habit of that! Welcome to the family, son."

Betsy wanted to know what Sallie was up to. Billy said, "She was shoeing her horse when we were over there, but she was about to finish that up."

"I'm going to give her a call and see if she'll come over for dinner tonight." With that, Betsy was off to try to reach her sister.

We walked around to the front and sat in our respective rockers. Somehow, while they were all the same around the different sides of the house, we each always sat in the same one every time. Bill called it "our favorite pew."

None of the three of us said a word before Betsy was back to report that Sallie was coming to dinner.

As evening approached, I couldn't help but notice that Betsy was going to extra lengths to make the evening special. I'm not much help in the kitchen unless you want a peanut butter fold-over, but I offered to do whatever I could. Used to giving "domestic help" orders, she told me step-by-step exactly how she wanted the table set, what she wanted set out on the bar, and where to find everything I'd need to fulfill the tasks. Bill was to be queued up to make old fashioneds when Sallie arrived as this was her favorite drink, which she partook one of only on very special occasions and two on Christmas Day. By then, Billy and I were to be serenading them with, as Betsy put it, "our better pieces—not 'Wall Street Bandidos'." Her main entree was Geermann-Schlatter prime rib.

When Bill walked through the room, he said, "Mother, your sister is going to think the year got away from her. The table looks like it's set for Christmas dinner."

"She's going to get her Christmas cocktails too. I want everything nice," she said as she went about methodically in the kitchen—cleaning things up as she went along, as was her habit.

That morning while Billy and I were out on our ride, Bill had loaded a broken gate into the back of his pickup, and he now asked Billy to go with him over to Sallie's to weld it. Once Betsy had things prepped in the kitchen as far as she could for the moment, and "signed off" on my table duties, she went to be alone in the chapel.

As I sat in the great room in one of the big leather chairs next to the fireplace, it occurred to me I'd never been alone in the house before—even during construction. The only noise was the ticking of the old grandfather clock that had belonged to Bill's mother and his grandmother before that.

Instead of feeling odd or lonely, it seemed incredibly peaceful. And with the feeling of peace, an even deeper sense that something was settling there with me. It was an overwhelming sense of dignity—not as some better-than-thou attitude. It was pure gift. The kind of dignity that you can't pursue or grab or claim to possess. It must be given freely and accepted freely. In that moment, I knew this was the gift given to me by these three people whose lives I had fallen into through fates beyond my wildest imaginings. Betsy was in the chapel much longer than usual. Bill and Billy were taking longer on the gate than I imagined it would take. I had a long time to be alone and still— there in the house that had opened a whole new chapter of my life.

As I studied the room, my mind took me to the hard labor that brought it forth. Ernesto, who always blared the radio in his truck, never allowed a radio on the jobsite. He wanted to be sure we *muchachas* could take his instruction without competition. That was certainly an important part of how he honed our skills as we went along, but I also knew it gave that badass the freedom to break into song whenever the spirit within called him forth to do so. I could hear again his voice singing the chorus of that famous Christmas song as he sang in Spanish, which, I believe in that moment, was his prayer of thanksgiving to his *mamá*.

Oh escuchad a los ángeles cantando
Oh noche divina,
noche cuando Jesús nació
Oh noche divina,
noche cuando Jesús nació

I looked again at the materials that made this house. In my mind I remembered, stapled to the legal pad that Bill and Betsy had given us was a picture of a tile floor with small diamond tiles in each corner where four tiles met. The note beside it read, "Wondering if we can do this with Saltillo with small two inch cobalt diamond accents."

I had said to Ernesto, "She is specific, isn't she? I've seen octagon and another shape or two but none quite like she has in mind. Can you order Saltillos shaped liked that?" And his answer, "Sure. All I have to do is order you to take every tile to the wet saw and cut off the corners." That was somewhat in jest as he needed me to help him. But the order was given—it went to Sergio who cut Saltillos for days. Now I look at the floor, and I see what is almost like a fine, classic carpet only it exudes all the warmth of Saltillos' imperfections and the radiance of its soft peach patina.

Imperfections abound. The tiles, the unplastered adobes, the round pine beams that rise up to the large ridge beam, covered by more pine and stained piece by piece by Manuel and Sergio. Ernesto handing them cans of stain saying, "*Chicas*, the first coat is this hazelnut. Rub it in good and then another coat on top of it. Then you take this coffee stain, thin it 50/50 and with a rag do a swipe over everything again. This will warm up the wood to go with the rock on the fireplace. Then, *chicas*, two more passes with satin sealer. That's all there is to it!"

There were no shortcuts working with Ernesto. He even said, no house he'd ever worked on did he ever push as hard as he did with this one. Like me, he felt connected to the healing that we were part of, and how much it was nurturing us in the process.

This house, now a home as few are, has none of the feel of mass production. It exudes the labor intensity and skill that accompanied that labor. In one respect, I could point to every tile, every adobe, and every piece of wood and point out some imperfection. Yet taken together, I'd be just as hard-pressed to point to anything that lacked care—that in its context isn't altogether whole and beautiful. I could think of nothing in the home where I thought "if only we had done this differently or better."

I was suddenly amused by the notion of Emma sitting across from me. "What do you think 'Dear Dad,' the critical perfectionist would make of this place?" I imagined her there, amused greatly, as she would recount how he would have to plaster over everything and sand smooth and paint it white—and cover up that floor with near-industrial-grade carpet. We would both agree that those stark white interiors so many people crave for their minimalist look are fine—and indeed a true reflection of the industrial economy in which most live. They are urbane and in context to their place—of a kind. This place would appear peculiar in such settings just as for me, the white, urbane minimalism would be out of context here on this spectacular ridge.

Here, imperfection is made whole by its context to place not in spite of it. All I could see as I sat there was an embrace of the warmth and beauty of a temporal building that will almost certainly outlive the temporal lives now lovingly enveloped within it.

I heard Bill's diesel truck as it neared the house and stepped outside the door as he cut the engine. Billy was in the back instead of the cab. I walked over to see what that was all about. Whatever it was, Bill was amused by it; I could see that. Billy, covered from head to foot in mud and shit looked up at me.

Bill said, "The boy had a little slip into a muck hole when we were putting the gate in place."

Billy just looked at me trying to decide if he was amused by it or not. So far it appeared not, though I couldn't hide my wide smile at the sight.

Then Bill said, "Come on son. I'll hose you down. There's no way your mother is going to let you in the house even to get to the shower covered like that."

Billy jumped off the bed of the truck smelling like a compost heap and finally smiled and said, "I think we need another big family hug about right now."

Bill said, "You ain't gonna find any takers on that, is he Jaime?"

I said, "I'm pretty sure we could get takers for chances to hose the boy down."

"No doubt—no doubt," Bill chuckled.

"I *will* remember this," Billy said.

While Billy was showering and getting back to his more well-kept self, Bill and I sat by the fireplace, and Betsy soon joined us on the couch. Betsy always thought Billy took too long showering and said, "There won't be any hot water left by the time he's done. You'd think living in the desert he'd be more inclined to saving water."

Being bad about that myself, I said nothing.

Bill asked, "Jaime, how do you think it's going to go with the Cardonas? You've been a part of their world for several years now. I'd hate to see you fall out with them."

I said, "As I've said to Billy, I've been a part of their world while at the same time not really—kind of an outsider always looking in, which is not to say I don't recognize the deep gratitude I owe to Chuy, Lupe, Ernesto and Rosalinda. For a time I had begun to feel that I was almost a stand-in for the children Chuy and Lupe never had, but I think that was as much my projection of wanting to be part of a family as anything. That's a rather winding way of saying, their family bond is so strong, I think they will bid me a kind farewell from the day-to-day life we've known together."

Bill said, "I hope you're right, and I think you are."

To that Betsy added, "If anyone will find the right words to tell them, it will be you—well, maybe you and the spirit that clearly knows when you need the right inspiration for the moment."

I said, "I'll take that both as the word of encouragement it is as well as the acknowledgement of whatever it is that guides me when I often least expect it."

Billy finally reappeared in the famous shirt he'd loaned me and in fresh-from-the-ironing-board jeans. His mother said, "Son, you forgot to brush your hair."

It was indeed a messy mop from towel drying it. Without a word he turned around and a few seconds later was back, all things now in order.

"What'd I miss?" he asked.

I said, "We were just speculating on the days ahead as I try to figure out how to tell the Cardonas."

Billy asked, "As Dad would say, 'Come to any profound conclusions?'"

I said, "Just that when the time comes, I'll open my mouth and see what comes out."

"That seems to work for you," Billy said.

Betsy surprised me when she said, "It doesn't work too well for your brother, Brett, as we have all noticed."

Bill wanted to offer me some reassurance and a little leeway. "Jaime, you need to do all this on your timeframe. It's not something you have to do Monday morning or the Monday after that. You do it how you want when you want. Your place here isn't going anywhere."

"I second that," Betsy said.

"Still, sooner sounds better than later," Billy suggested.

Chapter Thirty-nine

Sallie arrived right at 6:00 and was more "purdied-up" than I had ever seen her—not going so far as to wear a dress, which I speculated she hadn't done in decades—but dressed in black slacks and a deep red, long-sleeved blouse. She even had a little makeup on, which *really* surprised me.

Billy leaned over to me to say, "Mom must have told her to clean up for the occasion."

I asked Billy, "Do you think she knows it is an occasion and, if so, for what?"

He replied, "To the first question, absolutely. To the latter, your guess is as good as mine."

I said, "If we want our supper, we'd better get to playing for it."

Billy asked, "Shall we start with 'Wall Street *Bandidos*'?"

I didn't have to answer that question—it had been answered earlier in the day. And he didn't wait for an answer. He began an introduction on his harmonica to "Annie Laurie," which was my cue to strum softly along and start singing. Sallie had heard us sing in the chapel, so that was nothing new. She'd never heard us in the larger great room singing songs, which were clearly more to her genre of choice. She sat on one end of the couch, legs crossed, leaning with an elbow on the arm with her head resting on her hand. She had the contented look that comes when all is right in one's world.

Also on cue, Bill was there with a tray and four old fashioneds —giving the first to Sallie (who raised her eyebrows in clear approval), setting two down on the coffee table for us and settling into his chair with one for himself.

Billy had informed me earlier in the day, "Don't expect Sallie to help in the kitchen. She's about as helpful as you say you are, and Mom doesn't like anyone under her feet when she's got things in her own synchronicity—which truly is a gift she possesses in spades in her kitchen."

Billy and I would break between each song just long enough for someone to say something if they wanted or to just enjoy a moment of near silence—the only sounds coming from the kitchen part of the room, which had its own gentle, quiet rhythm and the softly ticking clock.

Sallie and Bill were a round ahead of us on the drinks, and when they'd about finished the second, we were all summoned to the table. We each carried with us what was left of our cocktail.

Bill was right about Sallie. As she went to sit in her usual spot she said, "Sister, did Christmas come early?"

Billy said afterward, "Mom must have worked out her answer to that question after what Dad had said earlier in the day."

Betsy answered, "Well, we did get a pretty big present earlier today, so it feels a little like Christmas."

"Would I be wrong to guess that it might have something to do with the workings of these ranches?" Sallie asked.

Billy said, "Yes, ma'am. We're fixin' to get one more body to do some work around here."

Sallie said, "As long as he doesn't pat any of our seasonal ranch hands on their butt, he should work into the job pretty well."

"I guess you've heard about the Slo Poke Cafe," Betsy said to her sister.

"I guess the whole county has," Sallie answered, amused at herself for bringing it up.

Bill asked, "Are we eatin' or talkin'?"

I was drafted by Betsy to say my one meal blessing.

Once we all had our plates filled, Sallie said, "I do have a little bit of news of my own. Bill, I took your advice and sat down with Vera to lay out what you'd set aside for her and how her retirement would look. I guess I didn't need to put that conversation off so long. She said, '*Oh, gracias Dios*! I'm so tired. My great niece says I can come live with her.'"

Besty broke into a full body laugh—I thought she was going to spit her food right across the table.

Bill asked, "Why is that so funny?"

Betsy said, "Mostly because you two have fretted about this for months for nothing, and partly because this afternoon in the chapel I said out loud to myself, 'If I were Vera I'd be itching for a way out.'"

Sallie obviously knew every detail of the plan. She said, "Boys, it looks like we might be swapping livin' quarters well before the snow flies."

Chapter Forty

The sublime weekend was over. The week ahead meant it was time to sort through how and when I was going to talk with the Cardonas. I couldn't imagine telling all four at once nor could I imagine juggling them one at a time. Ernesto, as my employer, should know before the others it seemed to me, but he also was going to spread the word faster than a West Texas spring wildfire when the grasslands are like dry straw and the winds are blowin' ya sideways. I had to laugh to myself that such a phrase even came into my mind. Clearly, I had acclimated to this place!

I didn't do anything about it on Monday or Tuesday. Bill encouraged me to take the time I needed. Betsy encouraged me to let the words come out when they were ready. Billy basically said, "Don't fart around."

Wednesday an opportunity presented itself that I suddenly realized could be perfect timing. Ernesto came to work all excited. The missionary priest—his youngest, "Pope Chuy I"—was coming on a furlough from Central America. He would be home for two weeks. Ernesto could hardly contain himself.

I got on the phone to the Schlatters. Bill answered. I asked if Betsy was there and if so it might be best to put me on speaker. Bill said, "They're both here," and Betsy and Billy asked in unison, "Did you tell them?"

"No, not yet," I said. "But I have a proposition. You remember Ernesto's youngest boy, *Jesus*, is a missionary in Central America. He's going to be home on furlough for two weeks starting next week. I was wondering if we could host something for the family out at the ranch—not for the whole Cardona clan, which can tally up to half of Fort Davis depending on who does the counting and the inviting—just Chuy, Lupe, and Ernesto and Rosalinda's immediate family, none of whom have seen the house he built."

Whether there was a silent nod-of-the-head vote, I couldn't say. All I got back was Bill saying, "Go for it."

Betsy said, "I can't think of any day in the next two weeks we couldn't make work."

"Great!" was all I said and hung up the phone.

Billy hadn't said anything. I had a notion, not entirely unlike my own, he didn't see how a party for *Jesus* got me any closer to telling them I was leaving—a fact he confirmed when I saw him on Friday when I returned to the ranch.

"I did sorta leave that part out," I said. "My enthusiasm for finally being able to invite them to something got ahead of my brain."

Billy said, "Mom and Dad didn't seem to notice or care. I guess they showed more faith than me that you knew what you were doing."

Then I laid out how things went once I hung up from that call. I said, "I got the mind and the enthusiasm stitched back together once I hung up. Ernesto was so excited about *Padre Jesús* coming home that I knew he'd be telling everyone in town—I'd be the last thing on his mind. I decided to tell him then and there, as well as let him know that Bill and Betsy wanted to have the family out to see the house while *Jesus* was home. Then when I was back at the casita after work, I'd tell Chuy and Lupe both about my move and the party at the ranch."

"And did you 'git 'er done' like that?" Billy asked.

"I'm getting there," I said. "I first offered the invitation for the party, which you could see Ernesto was happy about—eager to show off all his good work. I said, just pick a date. He said he'd check with Rosalinda who he would then have call Betsy to coordinate things. Then I said, 'I haven't told Lupe and Chuy yet— I plan to do that this evening—but Bill and Betsy have asked me to come work on the ranches as Sallie is wanting to wind down towards retirement.'

"He said with a big grin, '*Tu pendejo!*' Then he reached out his hand to shake mine and said, 'Rosalinda always said you were on loan. She didn't know why or what it meant. She just knew I had you while I had you and should be ready to say *adios* when the time came.

"Then he said how he wasn't going to work at all while young Chuy was home. He said we could wrap up the little we needed to get done this coming week, and if you are ready to have me, I could start Monday. He did ask me if I would still do any house plans or if I was giving that up. I told him I would still do those—at least I thought I would. I hadn't thought to bring that up when you and I talked. I was still in shock. Anyway, he said, 'I hope you will. We're getting a good reputation from them.'

"And my plan almost worked except that Ernesto called Rosalinda to tell her about the party and find out when she would want to schedule it. When I got back to the casita after work, Lupe and Chuy stepped outside their door as I got out of my truck, both with arms folded and an irritated look on their face. I knew they knew—whether from Rosalinda or Ernesto was the only question.

"Then Lupe broke into a smile and came quickly over to give me a hug. Chuy came and shook my hand like I'd just handed him a winning lotto ticket."

Billy interjected, "So they really *did* want to get rid of you—like Vera, '*Oh gracias Dios!*'"

"You're a mess," I said.

"But I'm your mess," he said.

I continued, "Then Lupe said, 'Rosalinda called me as soon as Ernesto called her. She wanted to confer on dates but also asked if I knew the Schlatters had offered you a job.'

"Of course, I wanted to say, 'They've offered me life,' but decided it wasn't the right thing to say to them. Rosalinda had told Lupe what she'd said to Ernesto—about me being on loan."

Having caught Billy up on the week, I brought us back to the present. "I have all my worldly possessions in my pickup. If you come help, we can get them in one trip. I went ahead and left the imaginary Chihuahua for the next tenant, whoever that might be."

Chapter Forty-one

After I'd extended the invitation on Wednesday, Rosalinda called Betsy on Thursday morning to discuss the family gathering out at the ranch. She also congratulated her on the hiring of their new ranch hand. Betsy told Bill that clearly the deed was done but that they'd let me be the one to tell Billy how it all transpired. As she recounted this to me on Friday evening, I thanked her.

Saturday week was to be the big day at the ranch. Rosalinda offered to make it a potluck gathering, but Betsy would hear nothing of the sort. Betsy was rather hoping for some catering help from the Slo Poke Cafe, which she was able to arrange. They couldn't help with servers, but they'd prepare plenty of food we just had to pick up Saturday right before their regular opening time. It was agreed that it would be a luncheon affair with people gathering around noonish. Bill warned that might be "Mexican time," a well-known phenomenon in Fort Davis, which could mean arrivals from one to even two o'clock—but probably not noon sharp. They were prepared for any such contingency.

Billy, Jean, Mary-Alice and I all said we'd serve and clean up—that Betsy didn't need to hire help or worry about that. Sallie said she wanted to come, which given her private nature surprised all of us. Bill had been over to her place on Friday morning, at which time Sallie said, "Vera has departed."

Bill said, "You make it sound like she's dead."

"Oh, I guess I do need to phrase that differently. She has gone to live with her great niece."

I spent the week leading up to the party—having moved in all three boxes of my worldly possessions, getting the first real taste of working with cattle, and trying to think what special thing I could do for Ernesto, Rosalinda, Chuy and Lupe come Saturday. So far I had no ideas, and Billy wasn't any help. You'd think after all these years of knowing them, a simple gift idea would be obvious. The only one I thought would be easy to shop for would be Ernesto. I could always get him a new drag outfit—though I knew I wasn't going to do that. While certainly no longer destitute as I was in the first weeks here, I still was careful with what I did have—never wanting to repeat my failures of the past. Both households had their own way of doing things, and trying to guess what they might use of a practical nature wasn't at all clear to me. Then on Wednesday, I had an idea.

I tracked down Billy. "Billy, I was wondering if you'd help me record a CD since I know they have CD players. You and I could play and sing mostly the songs we've written with your dad's words. We could fill it in with a couple of golden oldies I know from our nights sitting out at the casita that Chuy and Lupe really like."

Billy said, "That sounds like a really good idea."

We had never worried about missing a note here and there before, but since we were recording we wanted to get it right. Each song took several tries—working on it every evening—until by late Friday night we had all our tracks down and ready to give it to them at the party.

About midweek Bill recalled a conversation much earlier when he and I had first met about there being a Cardona mariachi band and he wondered about having them play. We all thought the crowd size might get out of control if we went that route.

Betsy said, "I'm sure people want music going all the time but you can't hear yourself think. I'd much rather you and the boys trade off playing a few things over the course of the afternoon."

Bill noted, "I'm not big on playing my mandolin for a crowd."

"Gifts should be shared," was all Betsy said, which in her mind, meant the matter was settled.

Billy asked, "You do remember Jaime and I are supposed to help serve, don't you?"

His mom replied, "If you can rustle cattle, you can rustle grub and music."

"There you have it!" I said.

Almost getting the last word as his mother went back inside, Billy mumbled, *"Jawohl, herr kommandant."*

As the door swung closed she said, "I heard that!"

Unbeknownst to any of us, including Betsy, Bill had talked with the Catholic priest in town, asking, "If one wanted to give a small donation to the mission young Chuy served, how would one go about it?" The priest himself wasn't sure but knew the bishop's office in El Paso would. Bill called them and got the specifics he needed. Rosalinda had told Billy and me at the food pantry about the extreme poverty where *Jesus* was. She said his missionary work was more about trying to help people exist from one day to the next than it was about celebrating Mass.

At dinner on Friday Bill wanted to "discuss it as a family." His intent was to give the diocese a check for $25,000 earmarked for the work in El Salvador where *Jesus* was serving.

He said, "The bishop assured me every dime would go there and that the bishop on that end was of the highest repute and could be trusted to spend it wisely on the most desperate needs in the area." Then he added, "Of course, these are oil royalties—not ranch funds I'm proposing we give away. I have no intention of making this a big public showing at the party. All in favor?"

I'd not seen a "family vote" before. I wondered in that instant if they'd voted me in. I wasn't sure if I was now a voting member or not.

Betsy and Billy in unison said, "Aye."

Bill said, "I didn't hear your vote, Jaime."

"I wasn't sure I should," I said. "My vote is 'Aye' as well."

"Motion carries," Bill said. "Meeting adjourned as soon as we're all done eating."

I said to Billy afterwards, "So, $25,000 is 'the small donation' he wanted to give. It sounds more like he didn't want the local priest getting any ideas for future funding."

"Bingo!" Billy responded.

Chapter Forty-two

Sallie volunteered me to ride along with her to Fort Davis to pick up the food at the Slo Poke Cafe on Saturday morning. Betsy found that quite amusing, while Billy was so curious as to why he could hardly stand it. I certainly had no clue but was fine with the plan.

Jean and Mary-Alice spent the night in the bunkhouse. They'd help out wherever they could. The original plan was they'd stop in Fort Davis to pick up the food on their way out. Sallie's pronouncement on Thursday of her plan with me altered their plans.

Bill was instructed earlier in the week to be prepared to get beer, water and sodas on ice as soon as he was through with his morning rounds on the ranch so things would be cold. He was also instructed to "lean heavy on water and sodas and not so heavy on beer." This could hardly be put down to prejudice—she was always most concerned about guests having to drive so far back into town. Her concern was one purely for the safety of her guests— her inherent instinct for gentility, which applied "wherever two or three are gathered."

Betsy asked me, as though I knew through some telepathic connection to the Cardonas, if the Catholics sing the doxology. I myself had only learned it from the Schlatters at our services in *La Capilla de la Rosa*. I said I had no idea—I'd never heard them sing it though I guessed young *Jesus* would probably know it, and our bunch could sing it as the blessing. If they knew it, they would naturally join in, it seemed to me.

"You and Billy kick it off when the time comes," she said.

I snapped to attention, *"Jawohl, herr kommandant!"*

I surprised myself as I realized I sounded *exactly* like Sergeant Schultz!

"Not you too!?" she said, shaking her head at me with a little smirk of a half smile.

"I won't make a habit of it."

She replied, "I didn't think you would, but it was cute this time. I may have to tell the kids you do a lot better Schultz than any of them ever did. "

She no sooner said that when I heard a truck and three toots of a horn. "That's Sallie," I said.

"Off to your big adventure," Betsy said.

I got in Sallie's truck, and she was back in her "go-on-errands" bib overalls. The "purdying up" was put away until the next occasion.

"How you doing?" she asked.

"Real good. And you?" I asked in return.

"Fine—fine." Then she asked, "Go ridin' any bulls yet now that you are a gen-u-ine cowboy?"

I answered, "I don't think me as a bull rider has any future in it. Maybe if I was younger."

She said, "It'll knock the hell out of your back. I wouldn't recommend it to anyone—though I would have liked to have seen my sister on one a time or two."

"Sisterly love," I said as we both chuckled.

"Sisterly love is right."

She was quiet just a minute when I suspected whatever brought her to volunteer me for this trip would be made known.

She started in. "I suppose you've heard that Vera has departed" —laughing as she said it. "Bill says that makes it sound like she's dead. Well, she's not. I'd never want this to get back to her, but in the few days she's been gone, I can't believe the trouble I was going through to be sure she had some little something to do. There was a time she kept the place going. Of course now, there is less to keep going. She was with us all the way back to when Momma and Daddy lived on the ranch and Bill and Betsy had just gotten hooked up. Nowadays, I don't eat much or mess much up, so I could have managed on my own for years. I feel like the last couple days I've been on vacation.

"Now you promise me, not even my sister will ever hear what I've just said about Vera. I'm not sure if Billy can keep his mouth shut or not. I'd just as soon not find out the hard way when he makes some pronouncement in the Slo Poke Cafe."

She didn't wait for me to promise but just went right on, trusting I would keep such a promise.

"My *God*, I love that boy! Billy's got the crazy side of our daddy in addition to looking just like him, and he's got the heart and soul of that daddy o' his. And he works slow and steady like an Amish draft horse in his prime—and he's kinda built like one too— muscles, big ass and all. I don't know where that hind end o' his comes from—some recessive gene, I suspect.

"I'm not the biggest prayer on the planet, but I've been prayin' for years that he'd find his way home.

"You're a good sport to let him carry on the way he does, but I can see it's all out of love. I've never been one to think love only comes in one way—prescribed by somebody else. It can be a lonely world when it doesn't need to be. Billy told me he was *mighty lonely* up on the big ranch. People all around and nobody to be close to. I think he's just making up for lost time and was *damn* lucky you showed up to draw and help build that house."

I was having a growing admiration for this independent soul who clearly steers away from labeling people as so many do to keep their "moral order" in proper check—overlooking the hypocrisy that so often lies in the shadows. This was the lesson Betsy learned the hard way, but she did have a heart big enough to dare to try—a heart I'm learning runs *deep* in this family.

I said, "I feel like I'm the one with all the luck."

Then she asked, "You ready to swap houses?"

I answered, "When that happens is entirely up to you."

She said, "I'd just as soon simplify and settle things sooner rather than later. I thought since you were the new kid on the block, I'd see if you're comfortable going right ahead with it. If you are, I'll talk to my sister."

"Fine by me," I said. "Hopefully, Billy too."

Looking straight down the road she chuckled, her head shaking gently back and forth, "You don't have to worry about that! 'Wither thou goest...he will go.'

"That's from the Old Testament in case you didn't know. I just swapped a pronoun to make it fit."

Chapter Forty-three

As noon approached on the day of the Cardona celebration for *Jesus*, I wondered if Bill would be right about an indefinite time of arrival. Ernesto was certainly habitually on time to work, and Chuy and I were always early to the tomato farm. Rosalinda was prompt *always* at the pantry. However, not having been included in their family gatherings other than Easter and the one time at Ernesto and Rosalinda's, I had no idea how they managed their social schedule. Noon came and went. Betsy had everything that would be served hot ready to come out on a moment's notice and the same for anything cold. Since I'd set the ball rolling on the affair, I rather hoped they'd arrive soon.

I was relieved when I saw half a dozen vehicles coming down the ranch road. The grandfather clock struck fifteen minutes past the hour.

Bill and Betsy welcomed their guests and made it clear all were welcome throughout the house and chapel to see Ernesto's fine work. The Reverend *Jesus* was in a black cassock and looked like he possessed a quiet, humble demeanor. I immediately thought— what a contrast between the gregarious father and his youngest son.

There were about as many cameras as people. Moments were being captured of the buildings, the views, and of all the delighted looks of the Cardona family. All Ernesto's children and grandchildren were there. We'd made it known that Elma could join Chuy and Lupe if she wanted to come. I realized how much smaller she had become in the years since that first Easter. She couldn't let herself come empty-handed. She and Lupe had made four dozen deviled eggs. I thought they might do something like that though I had no idea how many they might show up with. Betsy had designated "just the spot" where we servers were to set each plate as it was needed.

Ernesto got pulled this direction and that as members of the family wanted his picture next to different parts of the house, the chapel and the chapel wall.

I was even pulled into a couple myself—always at Ernesto's insistence. I said to him, "You're a rock star. Sign any autographs yet?"

He said, "The only signature this group wants from me is on the bottom of a check or a co-sign on a loan." He laughed and said, "Oh, then I hear, 'We love you *Papá!*'"

The oldest daughter heard him say it, and kissed him on the cheek repeating his words, "Oh, we love you *Papá!*"

Elma wanted her picture taken with Lupe in *La Capilla de la Rosa* —adorned now with the plaque that had arrived a few weeks earlier and Billy had hung next to the door as you entered.

Billy and I played a couple songs which, as we expected, no one was really listening to, but still they applauded of a kind when we ended each song. Billy said, "They're applauding because it ended!"

When Bill saw how little mind they paid to our playing, he decided this was a public performance he could handle.

He said to us, "I'll take it from here. Go help your mother."

He seemed to say it to both of us—and it must be said, Betsy had been more of a mother to me than the one who bore me. Of course, that is a *very* low bar and an insult to Betsy to even make the comparison.

We four assigned servers got to setting all the food out. Then Betsy had a little handbell that she handed to Sallie and said, "Go out and ring the daylights out o' this thing until they all come around the table."

I wished in that moment Sallie would have known Billy's "Hogan's Heroes" response when such commands are given. Instead she just said, "Yes, Sis."

Once people were more or less assembled but before they stood around wondering what came next exactly—Is there a prayer? Is there not? Do we just dig in?—Billy and I started the doxology as assigned.

Praise God, from whom all blessings flow;
Praise him, all creatures here below;
Praise him above, ye heav'nly host;
Praise Father, Son, and Holy Ghost.

To our good fortune, the big, beautiful voice of Ernesto jumped right in with us as the chorus grew across the family. Clearly, they knew it, and young *Jesus* took off in a tenor harmony soaring above the crowd as he stood right next to his ornery father whose mother had wanted her youngest to be a priest. Now her youngest grandson, in his cassock, was home for a respite from serving the destitute of El Salvador. My voice got so weak it began to crack, but my voice wasn't needed that day. I don't suppose my tears were either, but there wasn't a thing I could do about those.

With the blessing complete, the camera crowd was getting pictures of the long serving table with its abundance—before it would look like the locusts had descended, which it would in less than an hour's time.

I wanted four pictures that day. The first was a group shot of *Jesus* "Chuy" Alexandro Pablo Cardona the elder, *Jesus* "Pope Chuy I," Alexandro Pablo Cardona the younger, and Ernesto Julio Gabriel Cardona—the boy who never became the priest but was a good father. Then one of Chuy, Lupe, Elma and me; one of Ernesto, Rosalinda, Billy and me; and finally one of Bill, Betsy, *Jesus* and Billy. I knew people might not get what that last picture was about, but I thought *Jesus* should have it. The bishop had already let him know about the check the family had sent, and made it clear it was not to be common knowledge.

As far as we ever knew, *Jesus* never told any one of the generous gift to the sheep of his flock in El Salvador.

At the first opportunity when it looked liked Chuy, Lupe, Ernesto and Rosalinda were done eating, I summoned them into the house—into the sitting room in our small wing.

I said, "Billy helped me make a little something for you. Money-wise, it has no value. It is just a piece of plastic. Its value to me is beyond measure, because like this plastic, I arrived those years ago with no real value—a blank disk. Each of you recorded your lives into my memory until I was transformed. These songs represent the many milestones along that journey—a journey incomprehensible to me of how it could not have been possible without each of you."

As I handed them the CDs, I had a stark realization. I looked at Chuy and then at the guitar in the corner. "Oh my! You loaned me this guitar, and I've absconded with it!"

I started to put it in its case to give it back to him.

Chuy said, "That's yours—it's been yours all along. And whenever I listen to this CD, I want to imagine you are still plucking its strings and making music just because you can—just as you did sitting in your lawn chair outside our little casita."

Chapter Forty-four

It was moving day. Betsy wasn't keen on her sister bringing her old furniture over only to have to move her carefully sourced pieces from the new house to the old ranch house. Sallie, being oblivious to such things for the most part, was fine just bringing her personal items. She would use the bedroom I had been using for her office. The one concession on furniture was to put "my" bed in storage over at the old house and bring her desk, which belonged to their father, over to the new house. Betsy loved that old, hand-carved desk, so that took no arm-twisting. In total, our house swap took about an hour.

Sallie, Billy and I packed light. The marketed goods of "the economy" had no hold on our lives. There was not much more that we needed than a comfortable chair inside and another chair outside to take in the landscape or gaze off into the cosmos. And, of course, a musical instrument or two to go along with our voices when the mood to sing came upon us. Sallie had her own musical talent, though about the only time you ever heard it was if you happened up on her unexpectedly. She'd be singing away like some happy bird. I thought those curve-billed thrashers that called the old ranch house home were going to want to relocate next door. Those birds would be out looking for her—hoping she'd not yet departed to her final rest on the ridge with her momma and daddy. She and they had made the happy songs of that place for so many years. Maybe the birds would stay with us just out of habit. I hoped they would. Only time would tell.

Billy dropped on the couch that was Sallie's just moments earlier—head back, feet kicked straight out. "Oh, I'm exhausted! Here I thought we could really cut loose on our first night on our own!"

"I'm sure you did," I said. "Get up! We've got cattle to move."

"I'z the foreman around here!" he said.

"Best act like one then or your new employee will begin to think sloughing off is in the job description."

He replied, "You don't have a job description, that way I can change my mind whenever I might want."

"Tyranny," I said, "and I've hardly been under your rule a month!"

He still hadn't moved from his sprawled-out self on the couch as he looked around the room. "So what do you think of the old dump?"

I said, "I have two first impressions. As dumps go, most people would give their eye teeth for the good, old bones of this house—at least if they had any sense—and the second is no Chihuahua will need to give advance warning when turning around."

"Neither would a Great Dane," Billy said. "Do you want a dog or two?"

I had a strong notion regarding such an idea. "I don't want any other animal to care for until I know how to care for the ones we've already got! I know you know what you're doing, and I know you know I don't know shit!"

Then Billy said, "Note to self—cancel Chihuahua ordered for Jaime's Christmas present."

He added, "Here I was looking forward to getting a little pink tutu for her to wear when we carried her into the Slo Poke Cafe with us."

Then I said, "Note to self—order psychiatric evaluation for Billy's Christmas present."

Then he finally got up off the couch and ruffled his hair to look like a madman, and went hobbling across the room with his bottom lip stretched down on one side and his head shaking. He didn't say a word. I followed behind to see if this was an intro to an act, or if we were actually going to get to work. He was headed to the horses. I thought—the worker at heart can't sit idle for long.

Whatever gift I had for visualizing a house or picking up just the right stone that Ernesto was digging through a pile to find—there appeared to be no comparable gift for using a lasso. While it amused Billy, he and I both knew I was going to have to get the hang of it at some point. He made sure some time was carved out every day to work on it. Fortunately for me, he was a patient teacher. Unfortunately for him, I was a slow learner.

One time he saw my eyes were closed. "Does that help?" he asked.

"What?" I asked.

"Roping a steer with your eyes closed," he said.

I clarified the obvious, "I ain't roping a steer, I'm roping a hay bale."

He must have anticipated that answer because when he said, "It don't look like it to me," I opened my eyes to see he had moved the bale, and I was perfecting my warm-up before the toss to a target no longer there.

"Point made," I said. "I was just trying to get my mind programmed in a rhythm."

He said, "I'd let you do it that way if I thought it would help. So far with every toss you've come closer to catching your own neck than anything else."

"I don't guess I can say you make me nervous."

Billy intoned, "You'll have to do better than that. I put people at ease."

You could see he was pleased at having thought of that response. It is, of course, true, and was as true in this moment as any other. I thought maybe I just needed a new bull to rope. I gave the rope a couple loops above my head and aimed for him.

"Hot damn!" I exclaimed. "I got him! Hang on, you old bull. I'm pulling you in!"

Leave it to him to come up with a quick response that was quintessential Billy. "See, you just gotta want them steers as much as you want me!"

"You're a mess," I said.

"But I'm your mess," he replied.

I was decades behind the boy reared in the saddle and roping calves years before he could drive a car—well, at least one legally on the road. Bill had let the kids drive as soon as they could halfway see over the steering wheel—even as he had to take care of the pedals.

At least I wasn't totally useless. I'd worked with Ernesto and Roberto enough to have learned to be very handy. When I tried welding for the first time I did pretty well and could match Billy's welds in fairly short order. I was the better carpenter of the two.

When his mom asked Billy how things were going, he said, "Not too good. I was hopin' to be a housewife before too much longer but Jaime's cowboying has a long way to go."

Betsy just looked at me and shook her head.

Sallie was standing in the kitchen with Betsy and said, "Billy, if I knew you wanted to be a housewife you shoulda said. I coulda let Vera go a lot sooner and put you to work for me."

Billy said, "When you put it that way, it don't sound nearly so good. I saw how you worked Vera back in her prime. I don't think I coulda held up as long as she did. Besides, me being your housewife sounds like incest to me."

Betsy exclaimed, "Good grief! Jaime, take this boy back home. He's yours now!"

I grabbed his shirt sleeve and said, "Come on, boy. Enough excitement for one day."

Within a few weeks, I could see roping for me was starting to click. In its own way his silly, playful little line, "you just gotta want them steers as much as you want me," did actually change the way I was going about it all. I can't explain it exactly, but the magnetism that we'd shared as friends served as some kind of catalyst for how I began to approach the cattle—not just roping but how I looked at them altogether. It occurred to me how they moved in my mind—from a herd that all looked the same to having certain peculiarities and personalities that began to manifest themselves to me so it made it easier to "want them."

Well, I knew then, as good as the roping was coming along and as much as I loved the cattle, I was never gonna want them steers as much as I wanted our quirky, unconventional, and in so many ways, remarkable life together.

Chapter Forty-five

This wasn't my first Christmas on the ranch—that honor went back to that small gathering inside the just-roofed house when Billy first appeared in my life—and back into the lives of his family and the community. Little did I know then what I was in for—nor did the community for that matter. But this was my first Christmas since becoming a fully integrated member of the family. My first Christmas as a gen-u-ine ranch hand, almost approaching the competence of a West Texas cowboy—not yet there, but getting there.

Betsy hosted the first anniversary of her now-cherished Quiet Days that started that first Saturday in December. There was a small but loyal group who came every month. On occasion someone else might attend who generally had nice things to say about it afterwards, but who never returned. Maybe their usual routine on a Saturday was hard to give up. Maybe the quiet took their mind to places they were trying to drown out. Maybe the ranch was just too remote. Maybe it just wasn't their cup of tea. It did appeal to us—not just Betsy, but the whole of us. Not surprisingly, given her nature, Sallie was a natural. A little more surprising were Bill and Billy, who participated each month as well, though Bill spent most of his time of reflection either in his office or in whatever rocking chair might be open. We were hospitable enough to yield our "favorite pew" to whatever guest might have taken it before we had the chance to claim it as our own.

I thought how my one-time-professed atheist who had decided she preferred my notion that such a stance required a bit too much conviction—who in her last words said to sign her up in the church of mercy over judgment—would have been so comfortable at this "Christian" quiet day. Emma was a reflective soul, always lighthearted, witty and down to earth. Her gift was to see the needs around her—and unlike most of us—to do something about them. Claude was along for the ride so long as she was there. Once she was gone, he didn't see much point in hanging on. His time in the assisted-living center lasted about six months. I visited him on two occasions, but we never really could find much to talk about except Emma. It was the same conversation and same stories both times. Perhaps that was his mild senility guiding the conversation. Perhaps he'd just filed these as the few memories he didn't want to forget. I thought it most likely to be the latter.

I didn't know it until after the fact, but I was the only one in his file at the facility who was to be called when he died. I was not to be called for any other reason—those were his specific instructions. He didn't want to obligate me to show up if he happened to fall and break a hip or anything like that. So the two visits I made were merely out of my fondness for Emma and her telling me how close she and Claude had always been. When it was time, I drove up to get his ashes.

Billy and I drove to the overlook on the scenic loop—off in the distance across the vast valley was the majestic Blue Mountain. We had come here those few months earlier and scattered in the same spot, his loyal friend, companion and sister. I stood silently there for a few minutes when Billy came and he put his arm around my shoulder.

I said, "This may sound goofy, but it is as though I can hear her laughing as she says to me, 'Thank you for bringing him here. He'd have never managed on his own.' Isn't that crazy?"

Billy said, "No, I don't think it is. If that voice you hear doesn't come from some other realm, it for sure comes from what she planted inside you. I saw a real bond between you two, even though you didn't know each other that long or ever spend that much time together."

I said, "As far as that goes, nothing made her happier than seeing you and I together. She got the biggest kick out of you, and I think she knew I grew comfortable in my own skin because of you. I told her, I'm always telling you, 'You're a mess,' and you always say back to me, 'But I'm your mess,' and she thought that was *the* funniest thing."

Billy said, "I never said this at the time, but back when I went with you to see her in hospice, I thought—this is the first person I've seen face death so squarely. I'd sit there thinking, how many people's view to heaven is their evacuation plan from earth, but then are in total denial—scared to die? Emma had more the rancher's instinct that we take both life and death as they come. I should qualify that to say the rancher's instinct in our family anyway. I can't speak for any other ranchers."

I said, "For sure, she was not one to live in denial in any aspect of her life, right up to and including her death."

On this particular Quiet Day during this Christian season of Advent, I began writing—and by the end of the day had written four letters: one to each of those toxic strangers who bore me and one to the sad, angry brother and sister who, like me had been caught in their net. Given that the post office in California had a forwarding address for me—as soon as I got my PO box in Fort Davis—I had to assume they could have written to try to find me if they had wanted to do so. Possibly they waited too long and the mail forwarding had run out. More likely, it seemed to me, was that I'd not been missed. There was nothing to miss—that I had admitted to myself all those years ago.

These were not letters where I forgave them. Nor were these letters where I spelled out my grievances and wounds. These were not letters where I asked for any kind of forgiveness for my own failures or for anything that I might have ever done to hurt them. They were letters more suited to the very essence of our Quiet Days. They were quiet reflections on the abundance of life, freely given to anyone open to their gifts. My mind went to Bill's writing as I penned each line. As my hand moved across each page, I realized the four letters were love poems of a kind.

I dropped them in the mail on Monday—my PO box address up in the corner of the envelope. I would wait and see if one or more of them came back—return to sender, address unknown. None did. Thus far, none of them have written to let me know they received them. I would have only sadness for them if they still wallowed in the toxicity of the lives we all shared for all my early life. I wondered if each had received and read my letter—if it made them stop and think about what they could yet be open to, or if the letter was dismissed out of hand as though some creature from another planet had tried to communicate in an unintelligible language.

Before I sealed the envelopes, I let Billy read each letter. It was Quiet Day—we weren't supposed to talk unless necessary. As Jean always instructed people who attended for the first time, it is a quiet day—not a silent day. The idea was quiet reflection—not forced "monastic vows" of silence. But Billy was silent. When he finished all four he handed the four sheets of paper back to me. And a moment later, I saw something I'd not seen before and only entertained as a possibility—but was never sure—when we stood holding each other on the rock outcropping where we made our intentions known. He was weeping. I didn't know if he was weeping for them, for me, or for the years of separation from his own mother. Maybe all three. I thought about asking him afterwards but decided not to. If he wanted to talk about it we would. If he didn't, I would leave it alone.

It was the first time since I met this funny man, who amused me so often and so easily, that I was moved to want to weep for him whether he needed my tears or not. I'm sure that would make no sense to most people, but somehow it made sense to me in that moment. It was the realization that inside us is that place where wounds of the past reside, not to inflict their harm on us over and over—though many yield such a power to them—but as a kind of solace for us to understand how far we've come on the journey. I didn't weep for him with actual tears in that moment. It was very much a weeping within my own heart as, somehow, love had opened yet another door deep inside. It could be those letters and his tears had done the same for him.

Betsy rang the soothing bell—that Billy had made from cutting down an old acetylene tank—which was the call for each of the Quiet Day services and that she rang each Sunday when it was time to gather. She never rang the daylights out of it as she had instructed Sallie to do at the party with the handbell. She would take the leather strap on the leather-wrapped wooden clapper and slowly strike the bell with its gentle, resonate tone three times... then three times more...then three times more as we all moved slowly, silently into the chapel.

At this final gathering of the day, with my envelopes sealed and Billy sitting next to me, I remained completely silent even as they sang the usual Quiet Day closing hymn—which I always sing, but couldn't that day. I listened to the humble offering to love.

184

More love to Thee, oh Christ, more love to Thee!
Hear Thou the prayer I make on bended knee.
This is my earnest plea
More love, oh Christ, to Thee
More love to Thee, more love to Thee!

Once earthly joy I craved, sought peace and rest
Now Thee alone I seek, give what is best.
This all my prayer shall be
More love, oh Christ, to Thee
More love to Thee, more love to Thee!

Then shall my latest breath whisper Thy praise
This be the parting cry my heart shall raise
Still all my prayer shall be
More love, oh Christ, to Thee
More love to Thee, more love to Thee!
More love to Thee, more love to Thee!

Chapter Forty-six

The next day we had our customary Sunday morning chapel service. Jean and Mary-Alice spent Friday and Saturday in the bunkhouse. I asked Billy, now that we were in the old ranch house, if we should make it an open invitation for them to stay with us.

He said, "You guys fixed up the bunkhouse plenty adequately. I'd be afraid an invitation to stay over here might become a habit, and I'd just as soon not encourage bad habits—especially since Brett would assume he has the same rights and privileges."

"Good analysis," I replied.

At lunch after the service, Betsy announced that Billy and I were to go to one of the north faces where the stands of piñon pine are and get a nice big tree for the house. It didn't have to be on Monday—"but sooner rather than later" were her instructions. Sallie announced, if we didn't mind, she'd come along. We didn't mind and, in fact, welcomed her company.

Sallie trusted Billy so thoroughly with the care of her stock that we didn't really see that much of her. She had said, "I never got around to readin' much over all these years, and so I've got plenty of catchin' up to do." She'd settled very comfortably into her smaller world of our old quarters and spent her quiet days being her quiet self. Surprisingly, these days you were more apt to see her in slacks and a blouse instead of jeans or her bib overalls.

She and Betsy grew closer than they had ever been, though often you'd find them both just sitting in the same room, neither one talking, each head buried in a book. It was comical in a way. One would think of something to say, two sentences would pass between them, and then right back to whatever it was they were reading. It seemed to Billy and me that the temporary interruption couldn't have had any bearing on what it was they were reading. As different as they were in looks, often in dress and certainly in personalities—they were yet somehow mystically one—two halves lovingly put together again after years of some estrangement, an estrangement created by one ("under the influence" as Sallie would say of her sister's zealot days) and allowed by the other until she hoped it would pass.

We picked up Sallie on Monday morning to go tree cutting. She'd advised us on Sunday, "Every day you don't get it done will be another day you get a reminder not to forget." Sallie and Billy conferred on the best spot to go tree shopping, and Billy headed down the various ranch roads until we arrived at a gentle north slope with many of the bigger trees on the ranch.

We soon picked out a nice, ten-foot tree, loaded it up and headed back. As we carried it in, Sallie got the door opened while Billy was at one end and me at the other. Bill and Betsy were both in their big leather chairs by the fireplace with a good, strong fire going. Billy broke into song as he went through the door ahead of me.

We three queens of orient are
bearin' yer tree we've cut from afar.
Sap and needles, bugs and beetles —
Rattlesnakes left behind.

Bill and Betsy just sat there shaking their heads. Sallie asked, "I wonder how long he's been workin' on that?"

I said, "Not long enough."

"Tough crowd," Billy said. "I thought it was pretty good."

Bill added his two cents, "It was amusing. Such is your nature."

As we all proceeded to decorate the tree, the conversation turned to what to do on Christmas Eve. It was one of the few times during Betsy's fundamentalist days that she would forgo her own church's service and join Bill and the kids to attend the Methodist service. They'd done the same the last couple years. This year, Jean had wondered if they wanted to come to the service at the Episcopal Church. There seemed to be some question in the parents' minds if this was an invitation of obligation or merely an offer that was made this year out of consideration that perhaps it should have been made other years as well.

Sallie wasn't saying anything. I had sensed — and I thought the others may have as well (which was confirmed later) — that either the Methodist or Episcopalian option was probably going to leave Sallie home alone, as those packed service crowds were just not her thing. The last two years she'd quit going to the Methodist service.

That was easy enough when she was across on the other ranch. Now it seemed a little more abrupt somehow.

Billy offered his solution. "We three queens will decorate the chapel with evergreen and red poinsettias. We'll have candles and carols and everything merry. I say we celebrate Christmas Eve right here! Then, we can have plenty of spiked eggnog afterwards, and no one has to worry about driving late at night."

Sallie piped in, "If there's a vote, that gets my vote. And those in town who think I'm a teetotaler don't need to know that in addition to my celebratory old fashioneds, I don't mind some Christmas Eve eggnog with plenty of Jack Daniel's—just like my otherwise-dry, teetotalin' sister."

Bill said, "All in favor?"

Along with the others, I proclaimed, "Aye!"

Betsy let Jean know, and in case it was more an invitation of obligation, she used Sallie as their excuse. "She doesn't want to go to a crowded service in town," Betsy said. As it turned out, Jean seemed to want to skip Marfa in favor of the ranch as well.

"Is Brett going to be staying in the bunkhouse?" she asked.

Betsy said, "I've not heard if he is coming over Christmas or not."

"Book us in, if that's all right," Jean said.

Her mother assured her, "Of course, that's all right."

When Betsy told Billy and me of the new development, she said, "It could be you'll have to choose if you want to host the girls or Brett and whoever he comes in tow with. I'm sure you'll need to study which that might be."

Billy shocked me and his mother when he immediately responded, "We'll take Brett and whatever shows up with him. The girls have their advance reservation, and it should be honored. I'll be sure Jaime gets across to Brett that this is not to be considered a blanket reservation for anytime he wants to show up."

"Thanks a lot," I said. "We'll talk later as to that psychiatric evaluation we talked about giving you for Christmas."

Betsy noted, "I don't know what that's about, but you both may need one if he shows up with the wife and all his kids."

Then Billy put forth his logic on the matter, "They say ninety-somethin' percent of what people worry about never happens. I figure we've got only a one-in-ten shot of having to put him up."

His mother said, "How you arrived at your odds on this occasion is not too sound, but with your luck, he'll call and say he's already made plans with the wife's family."

Billy interjected, "She has a name."

Betsy clarified, "I was trying not to get attached, having made that mistake with the others. When they hit their fourth anniversary, I'll start calling her by her name."

Then I asked Billy, "Do you know it? What's her name?"

He laughed and said, "I thought I did, but I can't think of it at the moment."

I added, "I guess logical detachment runs in the family."

Chapter Forty-seven

Whenever we stop at the post office to pick up all the mail for the ranch, our routine is for Billy to drive to town and me to drive home. Since we do it only occasionally, there is generally a big tub's worth. He is the official mail sorter as he can ascertain much better than I what is important and what, if any, of the junk mail his mom, dad or Sallie might want. We don't drop it in the mailbox at the cattle guard when we retrieve the mail, they now get home delivery.

Generally, Billy just sorts. He doesn't start opening up anything until we're back home—just to avoid the mess in the truck. So when I heard an envelope being ripped open, I glanced to see what he had in his hands. It was a large, card-sized envelope.

"I can't believe it!" he exclaimed.

"What?" I asked.

"We've been invited to the Cardona New Year's Eve. It has a handwritten note from Ernesto and one from Rosalinda. Ernesto's says, 'Drag outfit guaranteed not to disappoint.' Rosalinda's says, 'You can see he's still hopeless. Hope you can come! No RSVP needed—just show up anytime after 7:00.'"

I said, "So 7:15 at the earliest."

Then crazy Billy said, "It doesn't say plus-one for each of us. What if we wanted to bring a girl with us? It's like they think we're coming as a couple."

"I can't imagine how they'd come to such a conclusion, can you?" I asked.

As usual, he was most amused by having thought of the plus-one "oversight" on their part. Then he said, "Too bad we didn't get this a little sooner. We could have ordered those kilts we talked about and gone at least as a matching set."

"Way too late for that," I said. "I guess we could go shopping in Alpine and look for matching sweaters."

I only hoped I was safe proposing such a notion—I certainly wasn't going to do it. It has already been hard enough for us not to look like the Bobbsey Twins since our builds—except for the well-known exception—are the same, and we wear almost indistinguishable clothes.   In fact our work shirts and jeans consist of one inventory, which we just divide between our closets when they come out of the dryer. Fortunately, no shopping for sweaters was ever done before the party.

Brett, along with his wife, Pamela (I did remember her name), and his four kids plus two of her three kids arrived two days after Christmas.   We'd been given a reprieve as the girls went back to Marfa to make room for "incoming."   Now, we lucked out a second time by not having to spend New Year's Eve with them.   Bill wondered if we thought anyone would notice if he went with us into town. Betsy noted it would be noticed both at home and at the Cardonas.

We figured Ernesto would answer the door.   What we might find was anyone's guess.   Indeed, he opened the door, but instead of his usual big smile he had a very serious facial expression.   It was part of the act.

I said, "Well, good evening, Reverend Mother!" He was dressed in a full Benedictine "penguin" outfit—the genuine article!

As we came through the door, he put his hands in "prayer form," bowed his head slightly to us and said to Billy as he entered, "Bless you, my child," and then to me, "Bless you, my child."

Rosalinda immediately pulled us aside.   "Can you believe it?" she asked—not expecting an answer. "Since we've not seen you in a while, you probably don't know that after Thanksgiving we flew to El Salvador to see Chuy.   Somehow the two of them got in their minds they should find an old nun's habit.   Unfortunately, it was way too easy to track one down.   When we packed, we didn't think much about it.   Customs on this end thought he was either some deviant or on the lam planning to go incognito at some point.   He told them it was mine—he was just carrying it for me, that I'd been a nun but denounced my vows because I was in love with him.   I couldn't tell if they believed him or knew it was such a good line of bullshit they should let him go. So here we are. I'll let you guess what song we're going to ring in the New Year with."

Chuy and Lupe were already there and came over to where we were talking with Rosalinda.   Lupe gave us a big hug, and Chuy gave us each a vigorous handshake.

191

"So you finally made it to the party!" Chuy exclaimed.

I said, "We've really looked forward to this." To Rosalinda I added, "Thank you so much for inviting us."

The three of them broke into laughter and Rosalinda waved Ernesto over our direction. She said, "Ernesto, *Jaime* thanked us for inviting him."

I asked, "Exactly, why is that so funny?"

Chuy explained, "The first year you were here, the party came before you joined us for Easter. You were still so quiet back then and reading those books by the monk that Lupe and I didn't think you'd want to be around all these people."

"That was true enough," I agreed.

He continued, "After that somehow, I guess we all just thought you'd show up and that one of us surely had mentioned it, which it turns out, we never had."

Ernesto interjected, "Chuy and Lupe asked me a couple months ago about it, asking if we'd ever invited you. I said, 'He lived with you! Didn't you ever invite him?'"

Lupe said, "When I heard that, we all started to laugh realizing we assumed you somehow knew you're a Cardona—you should be here! I told Rosalinda, 'Maybe you should send them an invitation.' She said, 'I could just tell them, but sending them an invitation will make it official after all these years.'"

Billy jumped in, "*Jaime*, what the hell? You were waiting on an engraved invitation when you were the holdup all along!"

"Too true. Too true," I said. "I never said I was bright."

Rosalinda added, "It will make a good story to tell your grandchildren."

Ernesto said, "Let's get this party on!" and he was off to greet the next people coming through the door.

As we were moving to mingle with the crowd, Rosalinda added, Rosalinda said, "See me before you leave."

Ernesto didn't disappoint. As midnight struck he raised his powerful voice singing "Climb Every Mountain." Once through he began again, having translated it, more or less, into Spanish. I say more or less as given even *my* level of bilingual skills, it seemed to me some *very* broad liberties were taken. Others clearly agreed, as numerous chuckles were heard from the crowd as he sang. When finished, he bowed to thunderous applause—including ours. The entire evening was a blast. And neither of us had ever been hugged on so much or laughed so hard in all our lives.

As requested, when it was time to head home we found Rosalinda, who took us back to their bedroom and closed the door, saying, "It's not some big secret—I'm just shutting out the noise."

She went to her dresser and got a manilla envelope. Handing it to Billy she said, "Chuy wanted us to bring this back and be sure your mom and dad got it. I'm not exactly sure why, other than I know Bill talked to Chuy at some length at the party you all hosted. Chuy keeps the picture of him and your family hanging in the waiting room of their new medical clinic."

Billy pulled out the picture to look at it. It was an 8 x 10 of Chuy standing with dozens of families in front of the village's brand new medical clinic—everyone smiling from ear to ear, no one's smile bigger than Chuy's. The large sign over the entrance read simply *Clínica de Esperanza*. Not that I needed to translate that for Billy, but I read it aloud, Clinic of Hope. It was all we could do not to cry, but we knew if we did, it might give away the significance of the picture. We knew the clinic was the place of hope the Schlatter gift had built.

On the drive home, I was thinking about Bill coming into the notion that he wanted to help Chuy down there in Central America. I'd remembered a line Betsy had read in the chapel that happened to coincide with the family's decision. I don't know anything about the man, but she gave credit where credit was due. His name was Frederick Buechner.

Where our deep gladness and the world's deep hunger meet, we hear a further call.

I knew Bill had heard the call.

Epilogue

How many times have I returned to that cowboy song I learned those years ago? I was little more than dried-up tumbleweed, blown to and fro with no notion of direction. No sense of call. Only simple dreams of a better life. But deep within there was a song, and it is here on this range that I belong. No longer drifting, I at last moved from despair to dreams to a life of joy—beyond the fullest measure of what I could imagine. The dark days of my past, now only a distant memory. Absolution given to the parents who bore me but never nurtured me. Absolution given to myself for all my own failures—the greatest of those being not seeing the light within.

If my years in California are to be viewed in a context of some meaning, it would be to say that they were loveless years. Not only did my family fail in loving, but I did no better. Dating and lusting are not love. Had my family not been so toxic, I might have snagged some poor woman who would have found soon enough that she had married an ungrounded fool with no capacity to know how to love.

Now, at best, I see myself on a journey—not yet having arrived at any real depth of being a loving person. I cannot judge others on this. They talk a great deal about love and how much they love. I hope it's true for them. When I hear them end their phone conversation saying, "I love you," I wonder, do they? I know they think they do. Is it that simple? Maybe it is. At least it plants the seed. That to my mind is worth consideration. But loving in some deep and perfect form is not yet fully true for me. At best, I am a suckling infant on love's benevolent breast.

I certainly know with confidence and deep conviction that I have a humble group of friends here—family of a kind—who I admire for their deep integrity, like very much for their acceptance of the world as it comes and am drawn to for the affection they give freely. Is that love? It's a start—I'm sure of that.

Chuy, Lupe, Ernesto, Rosalinda, Emma, Sallie—all woven into the fabric of my own coat of many colors—no allegiance to Pharaoh required. I was so blessed with inclusion, affection and care from so many from my first days here. Those years ago when I first arrived, I also could never have imagined how a broken family's healing would welcome me to heal *with* them—how Betsy, Bill and Billy would become the most important people in my life. If I do truly know how to love anyone, it would be these three. Once strangers who are now my family—and to borrow a line from Paul's letter to the Corinthians—and the greatest of these is Billy.

I was a child of a bitter divorce as so many children are. So often you look and wonder, as I had—was there any love there—ever? If so, where did it go wrong?

Here, I find myself, a straight man, still holding (much more loosely now it must be said) to the prescribed label—that one label, "straight," and a few others I suppose. All while living with this playful, witty, compassionate man who, like his Aunt Sallie, cares *nothing* about labels slapped on by others and has no desire to sit in the judgment seat cherished by so many who castigate others' souls to hell at every opportunity. Those judgmental, small lives are too hardened to see that such is *not* theirs to do. Bound up so long in the shackles they've forged, they are oblivious to them as they plod through life weighted down *so* unnecessarily.

What Billy and I have may not be a marriage, but it is an abundant life. And unless in my limited understanding of Jesus's teaching I have missed something, abundant life is the gift—the very point of life. Heaven in the here and now.

We had settled into our "heaven in the here and now" in the home Billy's mother had grown up in. The one, until Billy came home, that his aunt Sallie had assumed she would die in. Now, given over so willingly to the boy she loved so deeply, who loved her just as deeply in return—both so attuned to the natural world around them.

Once Sallie moved to the new house, she never mentioned anything in the way of regret about her move, though she missed her beloved birds.

She would often talk of the swallows that swoop around playfully in the day and then retire to their mud-packed huts at night. It amused her that they seemed to have to be next to every door on the place. She figured they have some particular need to see who is coming and going. When "Momma" and "Daddy" would come home with some vittles, and she'd see the chorus of chicks with mouths wide open, she'd say, "They look like Ernesto when he's in the mood to sing." Of course, the swallows left her every year well before the cold air set in, but they came back to the same nest every spring. Her father learned all those years ago that if he knocked the nest down, they would build it right back. For many this becomes an ongoing battle of wills. For Sallie, and now for us, it is peaceful coexistence. A little bird shit on the light fixture underneath doesn't ruin our day.

The curve-billed thrasher hasn't moved over to be with Sallie. The lovely bird retires early in the evening pronouncing her beautiful nightly benediction as the sun sets. She's up each morning to herald her satisfaction for being given another day. Sallie awaits the day when she will again hear the sweet songs morning and evening from her new quarters. For her, this is an article of faith. The question is not if the birds will come to her, but when.

Sallie figures the next time momma-bird thrasher hatches a few chicks, she'll send a young'un or two over there, now that she knows the house is all settled in. She was just waitin' to make sure the north wind off that ridge didn't blow the house over. Ernesto's good work has passed muster by now. Momma-bird'll be wantin' the family to claim the new territory before some riffraff bird gets the notion. I figure, if the riffraff does show up trying to claim the good nesting spot Sallie has in mind, she'll be out there with a broom.

We'd had a long, hard week—the kind of week when working the cattle would do in most men—yes, even those city gym-members, marathon runners, triathletes who fancy themselves tough and able to go any distance. We were worn out but felt a deep peace amongst all our tiredness and sore muscles and aching joints. We eeeeeased in—ever so slowly, so as not to offend any particular ligament—slooooowly stretching out on the two chaise lounges on the old ranch house patio.

Our evening companion, a cactus wren, was doing his usual chirping over on the yucca just to let us know all was well as best he could tell. I thought maybe he had just held up his "report" till then since we were late gettin' back home. I had never noticed if he chirped this late at night before or not. I knew he gets up early, but so do we.

Billy and I were in a rather deadpan mood. Too tired to laugh or cry or say much of anything. Just content to be.

We lay there barely breathing. Neither one of us snore. I couldn't tell if Billy was asleep or not. He was so quiet—maybe he was dead. I knew I wasn't. Every muscle seemed to be sending messages to my brain saying, "Memo to brain, we're all in this together."

A good ten or fifteen minutes passed...maybe longer. I wasn't falling asleep..."too somethin'" to do that just yet. I wasn't sure what that somethin' was. I'd have been content to doze off right there and wake up when the sun hit my face in the morning. Then from the chair just over to my right, I heard its occupant. He wasn't asleep either and hadn't departed this life. Not yet. I did know neither of us was in any hurry to depart, though like Emma, we didn't fear it.

We seemed to be thinking the same thing 'cause he mumbled, "I thought I'd be asleep by now...I was a little concerned about gettin' cold out here, though, 'fore mornin'...Maybe that's what's keepin' me awake."

I said, "I was thinkin' the same thing....That, and I can't roll around out here....I do a lot a rollin' around....one side to the other during the night....Can't do that on these chaises."

A minute later Billy said, "I'm the same way...Back when I figured I'd probably end up married someday, I figured I'd have to sleep alone anyhow if I didn't wanna get poked all night for keepin' the other'n awake."

"Me too," was all I said.

Since we weren't sleepin', I guess he figured we might as well talk a bit. He slowly, and raisin' his voice just above mumblin', said, "Since I was sixteen years old, I've done nothing but work my ass off."

I waited to see if there was more to that thought—apparently not. I responded, "Clearly, that is not true....As Rosalinda would say, 'Umm, umm, umm.'"

197

"Not my best analogy," he acknowledged.

A few more minutes had passed when he said, "Of a kind.... You use that expression quite a bit, and I've never heard anyone else ever use it....Where's that come from?"

I thought a minute. "I must have heard it or read it somewhere. I have no idea. It has a certain economy of words and broad use I just like."

He said, "You never do get long-winded."

"Not much point, is there?" I asked.

No answer came to that one—conserving words in the spirit of what just preceded it, I guess. Again we lay silent. I was gazing up into that Milky Way. I wondered if Billy was doing the same or was he over there with his eyelids closed and with his brain now on power-saving mode.

Then he said, "I can't remember ever getting into an argument with you...Have we argued?"

His slow pace of the conversation inspired me to do the same.

"We could think about whether we should have an argument or not...could be that's about to happen right now," I answered after a time.

"Do you think we'd enjoy it?" he asked.

"As I've witnessed some...they don't have much to recommend them....How about you? What do you think?" I asked.

He postulated, "Well...first we'd have to decide what we want to argue about...wouldn't we?"

I said, "I suppose."

He asked, "How about politics? Most people find a lot to argue about there."

"We agree on politics," I said.

"Then religion...everybody argues about religion," Billy stated matter-of-factly.

"As pertains to religion...what would you like to argue about in particular?" I asked.

There was a long pause.

"I can't think of anything offhand," he answered.

Without working at it too hard, he was still trying to come up with something we might argue about. His next idea came to him.

"Somebody's always gotta be right and the other guy wrong....
Do you think we could make somethin' of that?"

I had to ponder on that one a bit myself. "No, I don't see nothin' there to go after either....I ain't ever right and you ain't ever wrong....I guess that's why we get along."

He went quiet again. Still probably giving consideration to a topic to argue about one last try. I didn't come up with anything, and he didn't seem to either.

Finally I said, "Well, here's a thought...We could try this some other time when we're more in a mood to be disagreeable."

Then he asked, "Do we get in disagreeable moods?"

I said, "You're a mess."

"But I'm your mess," he said.

"Yes, you are, and I wouldn't have it any other way."